THE RIMROCKER

It was more than Shawn Starbuck had reckoned for. Unceasingly he had searched for his brother—a legacy at stake for them both—asking endless questions on numberless trails, in sun-baked towns, at desolate huts and sprawling ranches . . . and now it seemed, at long last, his searching would end.

Only it wasn't that simple. Suddenly there were three desperate men on the scene—cutthroats and renegades—each staunchly determined to see Starbuck dead. If they couldn't do the job, the richest man in the territory would hire gunslingers who could.

Starbuck had a choice. He could turn tail, clear out, and save his hide. But he wasn't the kind of man who dodged trouble—no matter what the odds.

Ray Hogan is an author who has inspired a loyal following over the years since he published his first Western novel *Ex-marshal* in 1956. Hogan was born in Willow Springs, Missouri, where his father was town marshal. At five the Hogan family moved to Albuquerque where Ray Hogan still lives in the foothills of the Sandia and Manzano mountains. His father was on the Albuquerque police force and, in later years, owned the Overland Hotel. It was while listening to his father and other old-timers tell tales from the past that Ray was inspired to recast these tales in fiction. From the beginning he did exhaustive research into the history and the people of the Old West and the walls of his study are lined with various firearms, spurs, pictures, books, and memorabilia, about all of which he can talk in dramatic detail. Among his most popular works are the series of books about Shawn Starbuck, a searcher in a quest for a lost brother, who has a clear sense of right and wrong and who is willing to stand up and be counted when it is a question of fairness or justice. His other major series is about lawman John Rye whose reputation has earned him the sobriquet The Doomsday Marshal. 'I've attempted to capture the courage and bravery of those men and women that lived out West and the dangers and problems they had to overcome,' Hogan once remarked. If his lawmen protagonists seem sometimes larger than life, it is because they are men of integrity, heroes who through grit of character and common sense are able to overcome the obstacles they encounter despite often overwhelming odds. This same grit of character can also be found in Hogan's heroines and, in *The Vengeance of Fortuna West*, Hogan wrote a gripping and totally believable account of a woman who takes up the badge and tracks the men who killed her lawman husband by ambush. No less intriguing in her way is Nellie Dupray, convicted of rustling in *The Glory Trail*. Above all, what is most impressive about Hogan's Western novels is the consistent quality with which each is crafted, the compelling depth of his characters, and his ability to juxtapose the complexities of human conflict into narratives always as intensely interesting as they are emotionally involving. His latest novel is *Soldier in Buckskin*.

THE RIMROCKER

Ray Hogan

GUNSMOKE

This hardback edition 2008
by BBC Audiobooks Ltd
by arrangement with
Golden West Literary Agency

ISBN 978 1 405 68209 1

British Library Cataloguing in Publication Data available.

Printed and bound in Great Britain by
Antony Rowe Ltd., Chippenham, Wiltshire

◎ 1 ◎

Shawn Starbuck halted in the shadowy depths of an oak thicket and studied the men. They were in a small clearing, and although it was not yet dark, had built a fire and begun preparations for the evening meal.

Three in the party. He looked beyond them, located their horses. Three also. That meant everyone was accounted for—not that it mattered particularly, but caution was a necessary ally in the world where a loner was always suspect.

Lean, much younger than his brow-hooded gray eyes indicated, he watched the men moving about their chores. For well over a year he had pursued his solitary quest, asking his question of every person encountered on the numberless trails, in the dusty, sunbaked towns, at desolate huts and at sprawling prosperous ranches. Here was another opportunity.

Thoughtful in the fading summer afternoon of the towering, hushed hills, he considered the party. Hard cases, all of them. No doubt of that. One, a ruddy-faced redhaired man, stood slightly apart, taking no hand in the camp chores as if above such menial tasks.

The second, at that moment hunkered before the fire slicing chunks of dried meat into a spider, appeared to be the youngest. He was thick-shouldered with dark, curly hair and a full moustache. The last was a much larger man than the others, fully six feet tall, of heavy build and with big, hamlike hands. All were dusty, travelworn—and armed.

It was difficult to think of his brother running with the likes of these, but then he really didn't know Ben—so he had no measure to go by. As in times before he had but one choice—ask.

"Ev'nin'."

At his bid for recognition, the men came to quick alert,

5

hands dropping to the pistols at their hips. Prodding his horse lightly, Shawn rode forward, elbows up, palms cupped on the horn of his saddle.

"Saw your fire. Figured I could bum a cup of coffee."

The men relaxed. Curlyhair resumed his slicing. The big one spat and settled back on his heels, evidently dismissing the newcomer as of no consequence. The redhead didn't stir, simply waited, watching with suspicious eyes as Shawn rode to the edge of the clearing and halted.

"Man could get himself shot sneaking up like that," the big one said, irritated.

"Been coming down that slope for ten minutes," Starbuck replied evenly. "You heard. All right if I get down?"

The two near the fire glanced at the redhead. He shrugged indifferently, nodded. "Suit yourself."

Shawn dismounted the chestnut and grunted wearily as his heels hit the ground. It had been a long day. "Name's Starbuck," he said, making an invitation of it. Sometimes the approach met introductions all around, other times silence or an outright snub.

"Names don't mean nothing," the big man said, "seeing as you ain't staying long." He reached for a tin cup, poured it full of steaming liquid from a blackened pot, and handed it to Shawn. "Here's yours. Slop it down and move on."

Temper stirred through Starbuck, hardened the line of his jaw as he accepted the cup.

"Obliged," he said quietly. "Except I can dig up a nickel to pay for the coffee if that'll help. Never like to put folks out any."

Curlyhair laughed. The big one stiffened angrily. "Keep your goddam nickel!" he snapped. "And don't you get smart with me, boy! I'll slap you around some."

"Simmer down, Rufe," the redhead murmured. He shifted his small, deep-set eyes to Shawn. "Where you riding, cowboy?"

"Little bit of everywhere. On the move most of the time —looking."

"For what?"

"M'brother. Thought maybe you might know him."

"Might," the redhead said. "He got a name?"

"Ben Starbuck," Shawn said, finishing off the coffee and setting the cup on the rocks near the fire. "Likely not going by that handle, though."

The redhead studied him in silence. Then, "What's he look like?"

"Not sure about that either. Been more'n ten years since

6

I saw him. Probably won't be as tall as me. Had dark hair and sort of blue eyes. Scar over the left one, but a man would have to look close to see it."

Rufe laughed. Curlyhair glanced up. "Hunting for somebody you don't know the name of or what he looks like. What kind of a yarn you handing us?"

"The truth," Shawn said. "Been combing this country for a long time. Important I find him."

Rufe cocked his head to one side slyly. "Take a right smart amount of cash to just go traipsing around here and there, looking and not working. . . . You must be one of then rich galoots from the east."

"Not me! Go busted pretty often and have to scare myself up a job, work for a spell. About to do that right now."

"We're busted flat and hunting work, too," the redhead said quickly, as if to ward off any hint that Starbuck throw in with them.

The man at the fire raised an arm, pointed to Shawn's belt buckle. "You ain't never going clear broke while you've got that."

Starbuck's hand dropped to his ornate, beautifully scrolled oblong silver buckle on which was mounted in carved ivory the figure of a man posed in the celebrated, crooked arm boxer's stance. Once it had been worn by Hiram Starbuck, the gift of admirers who appreciated his fighting skill.

"Reckon not, but I'd never part with it. Belonged to my pa. Came to me when he died."

"Sure mighty fancy," Curlyhair said. "This pa of yours —he a champion or something?"

"Was a farmer but he learned to be a boxer from an Englishman friend of his. Was never beat at it."

"You learn from him?"

"Some. . . . You sure you never run into anybody that could've been my brother?"

Rufe and Curlyhair shook their heads. The third man shrugged. "No more'n you've told us, we could've a hundred times. Description fits half the men in the country. There some extra special reason why you're so set on finding him?"

A most important reason, Shawn thought. As an heir of Hiram's, he must locate his brother or produce incontestable proof of his death. Otherwise the thirty thousand dollars lying in the vaults of an Ohio bank would go to charity, and his legacy of half would be lost.

It was a provision in Hiram Starbuck's will. Ben, who

7

ran away from home at sixteen rather than live under the iron-fisted rule of his father, had to be found so that he might receive his rightful share of the estate. It was the old man's way of saying he was sorry, and the lawyer had told Shawn there was no way of getting around it. But this was no matter for strangers' ears.

"Him being my brother—guess that's special enough. Folks are both dead now. He's all the kin I got."

"And you just aim to keep looking till you find him," Curlyhair said, eyes again on Shawn's buckle.

Starbuck nodded. "I'll find him."

Rufe grunted. "Plain loco, I'd say. No more'n you got to go on, you can hunt till you got a beard three foot long, and you probably won't run into him."

Again the redhead shrugged. "Luck," he murmured and turned to Curlyhair. "Pete, how's that stew coming?"

"Pretty soon," the younger man replied irritably. "Got to let it boil for a spell." He glanced at Rufe. "Would help some was you to get some more dry wood. . . . You know—I don't recollect ever signing up to be cook for this outfit!"

Rufe walked to the edge of the clearing and dragged back a fair-sized dead limb. Dropping it, he began to stomp the limbs, breaking them into short sticks. Scooping up an armload, he tossed them to Pete's side.

"That make you happy, Mister Brock?"

Curlyhair made no answer, but simply fed a handful of the wood to the flames and swung his attention to the redhead. "Starbuck eating with us? Have to add some water if—"

"Nope, best I be moving on," Shawn cut in before the man could reply. "Obliged just the same."

Whatever it was cooking didn't smell particularly appetizing. Besides, if he expected to reach the Underwood ranch sometime the next day, he'd best keep moving until full dark before halting for the night.

"Might as well hang around," Brock said. "We'll have plenty."

Starbuck shook his head, turned toward his horse. Pete's voice, almost insistent, reached him.

"We got us a pretty nice camping spot here, and you're sure welcome. Don't mind us none if we ain't been too polite. And Rufe ain't half bad, once you know him. Neither is Rutter. Just act that way to fool folks."

Shawn was conscious of Rutter's eyes upon him, sharp, suspicious. "Something about me bother you?"

"That gun you're packing," the other replied. "Don't look like no farmer's iron to me."

8

"Wasn't my pa's. Bought it myself, brand new, when I started hunting for Ben."

"From the looks of the handle, I'd say you've been using it right often," Rutter observed drily.

"Man learns," Starbuck said, equally dry.

Rufe slapped at his leg. "Man! Why, you ain't much more'n a slick-eared kid! I bet you ain't even eighteen yet."

"Old enough to wipe my own nose—and pick my friends," Shawn said, swinging into the saddle.

"And I'll bet you're sharp with that hogleg, too! Even wearing it left-handed! Whooo—ee! Boys, them's the worst kind—them killers that wears their iron on the left side!"

Pete Brock lifted his hands in mock alarm. "You think there's a chance he might be Billy the Kid or somebody 'stead of who he claims? Rufe, you sure better button your lip! Could get yourself in a peck of trouble—killed maybe."

"That's a fact," Rufe grinned. "I ain't saying no more."

Starbuck, only faintly stirred by the razzing, nodded. "Thanks for the coffee. You run into anybody who might be my brother, appreciate your mentioning that I'm looking for him."

Rutter's expression did not change. "Sure," he murmured. "We'll do that."

◎ 2 ◎

Starbuck never placed much confidence in such assurances, even those more convincing than Rutter's. Men forget when no personal interest is involved; Rutter and his two friends could come face to face with Ben that next day and likely make no connection unless, of course, the name Starbuck came up—and that was unlikely. Ben had long ago made it plain he was through with the family name.

Riding slowly down the slope, Shawn again relived the stormy scene that had taken place so far back now in the past. He recalled vividly the large kitchen of the farmhouse near the Muskingum River in Ohio; the squat, powerful figure and glowering features of his father; the tight, drawn face of Ben, fearful yet stubbornly defiant, like a young wolf at bay crouching near the doorway.

"I'm leaving, Pa! And I'm never coming back. Changing my name, too! Don't want anybody knowing you're my kin!"

"You ain't going nowhere, boy," the elder Starbuck had replied. "That licking was for your own good—what you earned for not doing what you was told."

"You always say that, and I'm tired of hearing it. You're not ever getting the chance to beat me again!"

Had their mother been alive there wouldn't have been that final confrontation, Shawn realized years later. Hiram Starbuck, despite his tough, brutal way, displayed a strange, almost childlike reverence for his wife, and while she lived he was not too hard on Ben.

Clare Starbuck had been a schoolteacher, and although her husband had had little patience with books, considering them a waste of good time that might be better spent working in the fields, he had deferred even to her wish that their sons acquire an education. And they did so;

10

partly in the schoolhouse in Muskingum, and partly through Clare's own efforts.

But when Clare died one winter, a victim of lung fever, a change came over Hiram and brought with it a deep bitterness that for some inexplicable reason focused upon the elder of the two sons. Ben accepted it stolidly for two years, and then rebelled.

As is often the case, the cause was minor: a hayrick that Ben had been told to cover before an impending rain storm. He had gotten busy at another chore and forgotten. Hiram, driving into the yard after a trip to town, noted the rick, and even though the rain had not arrived, flew into a rage, whipped Ben mercilessly.

And so the break came. Hiram never really believed that his son would leave, but he had been wrong. Ben, filled with grim outrage, had turned through the doorway and strode off down the road.

"He'll be coming back," Hiram had said. "And it'll be before morning."

But Ben didn't come back, and as the days passed into weeks, and the weeks changed into months, Shawn knew his brother never would. Ben had been that way: steadfast and determined like their mother, but equally strong and stubborn like their father. He'd cut his rope, and be it too short or too long, he'd make the best of it.

Things changed slightly after Ben's departure. Hiram, who had more or less ignored Shawn before, now turned his thoughts to the younger boy. But it was a less violent, less demanding attention; he actually became somewhat considerate and understanding, either because he had a deep fear of losing him also, or because he saw in Shawn a strong likeness to the woman he'd worshipped. Accordingly, life on the farm was somewhat easier for the boy.

Education, of course, had stopped that spring after Clare Starbuck's death, but Shawn had been quick to learn and accrued more in the way of formal knowledge than the average student; thus he felt no great heartache when he put aside his books for the last time.

Moreover, Hiram seemed to lose some of his zest for working. He hired two men to work the farm; and giving up his weekly boxing exhibitions in the ring they had built behind the general store in town, devoted those hours to instructing Shawn.

"Want you able to take care of yourself," he said once after they had completed a lengthy boxing lesson. "Reckon

11

you'll do that, too. You're quick moving, like your ma. And you got strength, like me."

Praise from Hiram Starbuck was something seldom heard, a jewel to be cherished; but the glitter dulled in the succeeding moment.

"You'll never be real good like Ben, though. He was a natural, that boy. An honest-to-God fighter."

Shawn had said nothing. Ben had always come first with their father; he guessed Ben always would.

That same day as they were washing up on the back porch of the house, Hiram had paused and looked at Shawn keenly.

"You figure he'll ever come home?"

"No, Pa," Shawn had answered. "He never will."

Hiram's square-jawed face, only slightly marked from all the years of bare knuckle contact, had remained intent as he studied his younger son.

"How about you? Aiming to follow him?"

Shawn had scrubbed thoughtfully at the dirt clinging to his arms—dirt ground into his hide when he had been knocked sprawling by one of his father's accurate blows. He'd have no trouble locating Ben if he wanted to leave, join up with him. Several times in the few weeks before his departure Ben had talked to Shawn about going west, to Texas and a town on the Mexican border called Laredo. He'd learned of it from a family named Yawkey who'd camped in the grove below the farm for several days. They had pulled up stakes in Pennsylvania and were heading southwest. Fortunes were being made by bringing cattle across the Mexican border and driving them north to Kansas markets. If a man didn't want to get in business for himself, he could always find a good job working for one of the big outfits. That's where Ben would be—with one of the big cattle companies.

But Shawn had never given much thought to leaving, perhaps because Hiram had not been too hard on him, and he looked upon the man more in awe than in fear; and very possibly, too, an unrecognized, deep-seated sense of loyalty was working below the surface.

"Reckon I'll stay, Pa," he'd replied. "Leastwise till I'm full grown and ready to strike out for myself."

"Which ain't going to be long. You're more'n most men now through the shoulders and arms. And you're talling up. Expect you'll reach six foot. Let's see, you'd be fifteen, maybe sixteen year now."

"Sixteen—almost."

"Sixteen. Sort of lost track of things, seems, since I lost

12

your ma. Well, you're old enough if you take the notion. And I reckon you're man enough—but you'd be a fool. I've got a fine place here. Worth a plenty of money, figuring what's laid aside in the bank."

"Wasn't thinking about that. Just aimed to stay around long as you needed—wanted me."

"Ben was a fool," Hiram went on, murmuring, not hearing. "Could all have been his."

"Only half, Pa," Shawn had said at once in one of the rare times he had contradicted. "Half's rightfully mine."

"Sure—that's what I mean. It'll be split between you two."

Hiram Starbuck hadn't meant it exactly that way, Shawn knew, but the knowledge hadn't bothered him.

A year later Hiram was dead, and with the approaching end he evidently still had Ben uppermost in his mind. His will directed the farm be sold and the money added to his savings.

This was then to be divided equally between his two sons. Shawn's responsibility would be to find his brother and bring him back to Muskingum where the lawyer handling the matter could be satisfied as to his identity. Should Ben be dead, legal proof would have to be produced.

Thus Hiram would have his way. Ben would return home, and the elder Starbuck, who had never learned how to lose at anything, would win again. It would seem, however, that Hiram was so busy being clever that he paid little attention to reality. For one thing Ben undoubtedly had stood by his threat and changed his name. Also, he had been gone well over ten years and his appearance would have altered considerably. He could have grown taller or thinner, or, as time matured him, even have come to take on his father's blocky physique. And as for identification marks, a small scar over one eye was really the only definite one Shawn had to go on. And Ben's present whereabouts? He knew that a family named Yawkey had been headed for a town called Laredo on the Texas-Mexico border, more than a thousand miles away—and that Ben had indicated he would be joining them.

And to compound the difficulties Hiram Starbuck had not thought to provide funds for the search. Possibly it was an oversight and unintentional. At any rate, the lawyer saw it that way and advanced two hundred dollars of Shawn's share of thirty thousand to outfit himself with.

And so Shawn had set out for Laredo where he encountered the first of his disappointments. The Yawkeys were still there—at least some of them. Yes, they remembered a young fellow; name of Ben, seems—or was it Jim? Anyway, he was the one they'd got acquainted with up in Ohio. . . .

Where was he? Lord only knowed! Folks moved around so a body just plain couldn't keep track of nothing. But he'd hung around for a spell and then gone on to California. Come back a year or so later, was on his way to Colorado—place he called Cripple Creek. Was going up there and try his hand at digging gold. Might still be there, too. Heard tell folks had done right well in that part of Colorado.

But Ben wasn't at Cripple Creek either. Shawn was told there was a man who sort of fit the description who'd done a little mining back in the hills. Had no luck and one day up and pulled out for Wyoming; said he was going back to cowpunching. . . . He was a plain fool, though; once or twice he put on a fist fight—"boxing exhibitions" he called them—in one of the saloons so's to raise a little eating money. Was a caution the way he danced around and beat up them other birds—some of them a lot bigger'n him, too! Could have made himself a living putting on them shows and not fooled around with punching cows. . . . Whereabouts in Wyoming? Rock Springs. . . .

It could have been Ben—it probably was; but Shawn was six days late. The fellow he was asking about worked for the Haycox outfit, the town marshal informed him. Gone now, about a week. Got in a fight with the ranch foreman and damn near beat him to death. Fellow was in the right, too, but the foreman was Haycox's brother-in-law, so there just wasn't nothing for the fellow to do but ride on.

The marshal couldn't recall his name. Could've been Ben, or Dan, and the men at Haycox's knew him as Tex, but the lawman was pretty sure it was the right man; he did have a scar over one eye. . . . Was *he* looking for him he'd head for Dodge City. . . . Punchers on the loose all seem to light out for there. . . . But Ben wasn't in Dodge. There was a rider, though, who—

So it began, and so it went; often close, but always not quite, and during those passing months Shawn grew taller, leaned out into a big-shouldered man with cool, blue eyes that belied the youthfulness of his features and his years. He changed inwardly and a remoteness born of patience grew in him; and while there was friendliness for those who were congenial, there was also a quiet reserve that no one ever succeeded in penetrating.

14

He became a wanderer, drifting ceaselessly, halting only when he ran out of money and was forced to take employment. He learned as he went, acquiring knowledge and experience, but never losing sight of purpose: find Ben.

It was a disheartening, discouraging task made endurable only by the restlessness of youth; but Shawn Starbuck never thought of that: he thought only of the day when he would encounter his brother and the quest would end.

He'd take his share and build himself a ranch, he had decided. At first he had made no plans, being unsure just what he did want to do with his half of the money. But now he knew; a ranch—a fine one. Maybe Ben would want to throw in with him. Together, cash pooled, they could have one of the best. He knew where there was good land to be had, land where grass stood knee high the year around and there was always plenty of water—

But first: find Ben.

A practical streak inherited from his schoolteacher mother always interrupted such dreams when they began to captivate him, set his pulse to racing. . . . Find Ben. . . . That came first—

He glanced to the undulating horizon in the west. The sun was well below it now, and darkness was closing in fast. Time to be looking for a suitable camp site. Raising himself in the stirrups, he glanced around. He was about midway on a long hillside.

Everywhere was scrub oak, twisted cedars, an occasional piñon laden with sticky, nut-filled cones. No darker green band of growth indicated the presence of a stream or spring. It would have to be a dry camp, but that was not unusual, nor was it a problem. He had learned to carry an ample supply of water in two canteens in his passage across the arid west, and both were still well-filled from his last stop. He'd see to the chestnut's needs from one of them.

A small break in the brush appeared before him. He rode his horse into the clearing and swung down. For a time he stood in silence, listening into the falling night, alert for any sounds that would warn him of the presence of others. There was only the clicking of insects, the faraway mourning of a dove. Satisfied, he began to pull his gear off the gelding, lay it aside. The big, red horse was in fine condition, just as he always seemed at the end of a day. Shawn had made a smart trade that day in Abilene when he'd swapped the old mare he'd started out on for the chestnut—even if it had taken his last dollar.

"Ain't the fastest thing on legs," the down-on-his-luck

15

cowpuncher who owned him had said. "But you ain't never coming across one with more bottom."

It had been true. Parting with the mare, last tangible symbol of home on the Muskingum, had not been easy, but Shawn knew a long, hard trail lay ahead—all in a country where a good horse was a man's most important possession, and thus the exchange was made. The tall, white-stockinged gelding had never given him cause to regret it.

When the animal had been picketed outside the clearing, watered, and given the last of the grain carried as reserve against the all too many times when no natural feed was available, Starbuck got down to preparing his own meal. He was low on grub, too, and if things had felt right back in the camp with Rutter, Pete Brock, and the big one called Rufe, he would have put in the night there, contributing what he had in food to make the meal complete. But he'd learned to judge men well, and there was something about the trio that hadn't set right with him.

It mattered little, anyway. Tomorrow he'd locate the Underwood ranch and there restock his supplies if he discovered he'd reached another dead end.

Dead end. . . . How many had there been since he'd ridden out to find Ben? How many false leads? How many times had he pulled hopefully into a town or a ranch or a homestead, certain that he'd reached the end of his quest, only to meet with disappointment?

So many times that surging expectancy and soaring anticipation no longer moved him. Now, when he reached a goal where his brother might be, he approached with a quiet caution, almost a reluctance, and always with the thought: *don't get all fired up—wait and see,* uppermost in his mind. He'd learned it was better that way. Somehow the keen edge of disappointment was blunted.

Underwood's could prove to be like all the others. A cattle buyer in Wichita had heard Shawn ask his question of a bartender in a saloon and had spoken up: the trail boss for a rancher named Underwood sort of matched the description, such as it was, of Ben. Underwood's spread was over New Mexico way, up in the northeastern part. Somewhere near the South Canadian River. . . .

Big place, the cattle buyer had assured him. Be no trouble locating it. . . . Underwood used the Sunrise brand—a circle with four bars sticking up from the top. . . . Man could spot his cattle anywhere. . . . Might pay to have a look—talk with the trail boss, if he didn't mind the long ride. . . .

Shawn didn't. He never turned away from a possibility, even if it meant backtracking over trails he'd just traveled. There was always the chance—and this time it was better than a good possibility. Ben had been good with livestock, and likely had developed into pretty much of a leader where men were concerned. Starbuck had headed west that next day—and now, tomorrow, he'd know he'd either find the end of the trail, or the beginning of another one.

After his meal of bacon, fried potatoes, grease-soaked hardtack and black coffee, Shawn stretched out on his blankets and stared up into the star-littered, velvet sky. The dove was mourning again, and from somewhere close by an owl hooted peevishly.

Sometimes the weariness of the search, the loneliness of the trails, drilled deep into his bones. . . . Sometimes it all seemed so hopeless. Ben was everywhere—nowhere; Ben could be dead, buried under another name. . . . And, wanderer, drifter that Shawn had become, he could waste an entire lifetime—end up with nothing.

Not entirely. . . . He'd been a lot of places, met a lot of people—some good, some bad, and from all of them he'd learned something. That had value. Like the gunslinger he'd helped out of a jam. He'd really found out how to use a pistol from him—how to bring it up fast and smooth and at the same time preserve accuracy. *Left-handed man's got an edge*, Allison—the gunslinger—had told him. . . . And then there was that lawman in Wyoming who had befriended him. . . .

The dry crack of a dead branch brought Starbuck from a sound sleep. Motionless, eyelids only slightly cracked to give the impression he was not yet awake, he strained to locate the intruder. It was near first light, still too dark to distinguish much in the shadows. He could see nothing.

But there *was* something—someone out there. Indians? He discarded the thought. In this area there were only pueblo tribes, mostly farmers. No, it wouldn't be Indians.

Abruptly he tensed. A figure stepped from the fringe of brush directly opposite into the clearing. Pete Brock. Shawn's fingers sought and found the pistol lying beside him under his blanket. Continuing to hold himself rigid, he watched Brock, curly hair straggling down over his forehead, cross and halt before him. A hard grin was on the man's lips as he drew back his leg and delivered a kick to Starbuck's feet.

Shawn raised himself to a sitting position. Being awake, Brock's actions did not startle him.

"What the hell do you want?" he asked coldly.

17

Pete's grin widened. "Why, I just dropped by for that there buckle you're wearing. Took a real fancy to it."

Starbuck swept the blanket aside, sprang upright in a single motion. Right fist cocked, left hand holding his pistol, he faced Brock.

"Move on," he said in a low voice. "Only thing you'll get from me is trouble."

In that same instant Shawn heard the rustle of brush behind him. Alarm shot through him. He started to jerk to one side, wheel. In the next fragment of time he felt himself falling as solid pain and exploding lights overpowered his consciousness.

◎ 3 ◎

Starbuck fought his way back from what seemed a deep pit. Sharp knives stabbed at his brain and a mist swirled about him in thick layers. He stirred, shook his head. The mist began to fade but there was no lessening of the pain. Somebody—either Rutter or Rufe—had handed him one hell of a wallop from behind with a pistol butt or a club while Pete Brock held his attention.

He swore angrily, rolled over, sat up. The abrupt motion sent a wave of giddiness rushing through him. Fixed, eyes closed, he hung there, waited for it to pass. The world stopped spinning; slowly, he raised his head, looked around.

Two lean, gray wolves waiting stolidly at the edge of the clearing came warily to their feet. Tails drooped, heads slung low, they considered him through agatehard yellow eyes and then slunk off into the brush.

Starbuck grinned humorlessly, muttered: "Not this time, damn you," and pulled himself to his feet.

He stood there, a tall, swaying shape in the clear, raw light of early dawn, until his senses once more ceased their gyrations, and then took stock. The buckle—belt with it —was gone. His pockets had been turned inside out. Except for the clasp knife he'd carried since a small boy, he'd been picked clean.

Not entirely. . . . He saw his forty-five then. It lay under the edge of his blanket, only a part of the butt visible. And he wasn't broke. The twenty-dollar gold piece he carried as reserve was in its secret pocket sewed inside his shirt.

That wasn't important—the buckle was, along with the fact that he'd been set upon, slugged, and left for dead on the mountainside.

Grim, he retrieved the pistol, thrust it under the waistband of his pants. Walking quickly, he crossed to where the chestnut waited in the brush and led him back into the clearing. Saddling and bridling the horse, he collected his possessions (he had found his holster in a clump of rabbit brush where it had been tossed after being removed from the belt) and stowed them in their customary places; he mounted and rode out. Breakfast could wait. He was too worked up to delay.

Circling the clearing, he located the spot where their horses—at least two of them—had been hidden, and later where they had moved off, striking due west. That brought a grunt of satisfaction from Starbuck's set lips and he cut the chestnut onto the outlaws' trail. They had an hour, perhaps two, on him, but that meant nothing; he'd run them down if it meant tracking them all the way to Mexico.

They had left an open trail, making no effort to conceal hoofprints. Probably figured him dead, or else that he wouldn't be fool enough to come after them—one against three: a slick-eared kid, as Rufe had put it, taking on three hardened men. The corners of his mouth tightened. Rufe would learn—the odds meant nothing.

He rode steadily down. Soon the sun broke over the rim of hills behind him, and began to spread its light and warmness through the brush, across the flats, into the deep washes and sandy-bottomed arroyos. Rocks began to gleam dully under the brightening rays, prepared to resume their endless chore of gathering heat during the day only to surrender it when night again fell.

A brown and gray cottontail scampered out from beneath the chestnut's hooves, causing the big horse to throw back his head and shy to the side. Shawn had a second glimpse of the wolf pair, still lurking about, not entirely ready to give up on what had appeared to be an easy prey.

He reached the foot of the slope, halted, and looked out upon the wide mesa lying before him. It was almost level with only a short rise lifting here and there to break the grass-covered, tablelike expanse. No riders were in sight. Impatiently Starbuck swore. He hadn't thought he was that far behind the three men. Evidently he'd been unconscious longer than he figured.

Spurring the gelding, he broke out of the fringe of mountain mahogany in which he had paused, moved onto the flat, eyes once more on the ground as he searched for tracks. It wasn't going to be easy here; the country had enjoyed a wet spring and the grass was thick, spongy. Hoofprints would be hard to spot, harder yet to follow.

But eventually he found where three riders had de-

scended the slope, still heading west, and assuming they
would continue to follow such course at least until they
reached the dark green band of trees on the far side, he
urged the gelding to a lope and headed for that distant
point.

An hour later he rode up to the trees, found them bor-
dering a small stream that wound off north and south in
an aimless, carefree fashion. He located the tracks of the
outlaw's horses some time after that, having had to search
both up and down stream before discovering what he
sought. They had entered the water, and Starbuck, in almost their exact marks, followed, crossed over. There he
halted, puzzled, a deep frown on his face. There were no
signs indicating where the men had emerged. And then the
answer came to him: the riders were keeping their horses
in the stream, were now deliberately wiping out their trail.
That could mean only one thing; they had spotted him.

Silent and simmering, he studied the soft ground along
the stream. Which way had they gone—up or down? It
was anybody's guess. Keeping close to the edge of the
creek, he rode against the current for a mile or so, found
no trace. Reversing, he headed the gelding back with the
flow. After a similar distance below his original starting
point, he once again halted. He'd met with no better success.

Hooking a leg over the saddlehorn, he stared out over
the land now beginning to shimmer with the steadily rising
heat. There was no doubt in his mind: they had seen him,
and they were doing everything possible to lose him.
Something had forced them to change their minds.

He wasted no effort endeavoring to figure out what such
might be, gave his consideration instead to wondering
where they could have gone. Had they mentioned any des-
tination during the time he was in their camp? He could
recall none. They had been low on grub. . . . It was logical to assume they'd head for the nearest town.

Shawn picked his mind for some knowledge of the
country. Was Taos near? He seemed to recall that it was
pretty far north and somewhat west of that particular
area. Santa Fe? The old settlement that marked the end of
the Trail was due west, he was certain. . . . They could be
going there.

Las Vegas. It dawned on him suddenly. Las Vegas was
a good, live town, he'd heard, and it lay well this side of
Santa Fe. Since it was closer, they undoubtedly would
make for it. Immediately he settled into his saddle and
pulled away from the creek, aiming the chestnut for a

long bank of low buttes in the distance. He had no idea how far away the town would be—sixty, seventy miles, possibly more. But it didn't matter; that's where the outlaws would go.

He'd have to ignore Underwood's ranch and the possibility of finding Ben there, for the time being. Starbuck shook his head in irritation. He didn't like the thought of passing up the opportunity, but on the other hand another day or two could hardly make any difference. Underwood's trail boss was not likely to disappear in that short a time.

He reached the bluffs and began a slow climb up a steep wash to the crest. No grass grew here. The sterile, rock-studded ground afforded life only for a scattering of globular clumps of snakeweed and yellow-flowered groundsel, little else.

The chestnut found the grade difficult. Halfway up Shawn dismounted and went on foot, leading the big horse with a slack rein so that he could pick his own way. They crested the rugged formation, came onto a flat, halted. A dozen yards back from the rim, a rider slouched in his saddle, sweat-stained hat brushed to the back of his head, watching their arrival with lazy interest.

"Howdy," he said, shifting to one side. "All that racket you was making, I figured maybe a whole passel of mustangs was coming up the draw."

Starbuck swung onto the gelding, rode forward. "Hard climb," he commented.

"Can't fault you there. . . . You know where you're at, friend?"

"New Mexico—not much else. It make a difference?"

"Some. This here's Underwood range. We're a mite touchy about strangers riding across it, and plenty interested in where they're going."

A stir of surprise moved Shawn. "Was looking for the Underwood place. Didn't know I found it."

The old puncher plucked at his tobacco-stained moustache. "You got business with Sam?"

"In a way. Aim to ask about a man working for him. First off, however, I've got to catch up with three jaspers who owe me. Figure they came this direction. You see them?"

The older man eyed Starbuck shrewdly. "Owe you, eh? No, ain't seen nobody this morning but you."

"Likely heading for Las Vegas. It on west of us?"

"Vegas? Well, sort of. A bit south, maybe. . . . This

22

fellow you're aiming to ask Sam Underwood about—what's his name?"

"Ben Starbuck, but he'll be going by something else."

"Starbuck sure ain't familiar. Best thing you can do is forget Sam, talk to Tom Gage. He's ramrodding the outfit. Does all the hiring and firing."

Shawn nodded. "Obliged. I'll drop back and see him after I've taken care of this other business in—"

"If you're aiming to go to Vegas, you'll be riding right by the ranch. Road cuts across Underwood's property."

That was a bit of good luck. Starbuck said: "Fine. How's the quickest way to get there?"

The puncher twisted around, spat a stream of brown juice at a nearby rock, and pointed to a dark, cone-shaped hill in the distance.

"Just you set your sights on that. You'll run smack-dab into Underwood's."

Shawn thanked the man and rode on. He was beginning to feel hunger now and considered briefly the idea of halting, brewing himself some coffee and eating the last of his supplies. But the prospect of soon reaching the Underwood ranch, meeting with the man who could be Ben, washed all thought of that away. He could hold out.

Close onto midday, with the sun bearing down full strength, he reached the end of the mesa across which he was riding and looked down into a broad, green swale. A cluster of well-kept buildings surrounded by large trees lay in exact center. This would be Underwood's.

Spurring the chestnut, he came off the plateau, followed out a narrow arroyo and entered a clearly defined road that led up to the gate. He cut into the yard, angling toward a long, barracks-type structure that lay to the right and somewhat beyond the main house. That would be the crew's quarters, and if Gage, the foreman, was around and not on the range, he most likely would be found there.

Passing to the right of the first building, Shawn glanced to the corrals ahead, noted the several horses lazing in the sun. At that moment a door slammed, drew his attention. A thin, elderly man stiffly erect, with a sharp face and thick moustache, came from a side entrance of the house, advanced to the center of the yard, and halted. Either Underwood or Tom Gage, Shawn guessed.

Veering the chestnut, Starbuck angled toward the older man, conscious of a cold, hostile scrutiny from small, intensely blue eyes. Pulling to a halt before him, Shawn started to speak but was silenced by a question.

"You another one of them looking for Sam?"

23

There was impatience in the voice. This would be Gage, Shawn decided, and irritated for some reason.

"Looking mostly for you," he began, and then his jaw clamped shut as the bunkhouse screen door opened and three men moved into the yard. He forgot everything else in a sudden surge of anger as he instantly spurred the gelding forward; he leaped from the saddle in a low dive for the man in the center of the trio—Brock.

◎ 4 ◎

Starbuck's outstretched arms wrapped around Brock
while he was still in mid-air. They went down in a driving
wedge, bowling Rufe over as they collided with him. Rutter shouted a curse, springing back beyond reach of the
struggling men.

Brock, on the bottom, took the brunt of the fall. Wind
gushed from his mouth and his eyes rolled wildly. Shawn,
jerking aside, bounded to his feet. Seizing the gasping man
by the shirt front, he yanked him upright, knocked him
sprawling with a hard blow to the chin.

Rufe muttered something, closed in from behind. Shawn
pivoted fast, fell into a cocked stance. He jabbed with his
left, rocked the big man off balance, and then in the
smooth, lightning-fast manner that Hiram Starbuck had
taught him, crossed with a whistling right.

Starbuck's balled fist caught the outlaw flush on the jaw.
Rufe stalled, a surprised look filling his eyes while the
muscles of his face sagged. His mouth fell open, and taking an uncertain step backwards, he went down.

Shawn spun back to Pete. A fist met him before he had
completely turned, jarred him to his heels. He shook off
the effects of the blow, lowered his head and moved into
the spinning dust stirred up by their scuffling boots. Pete
Brock was a confidently grinning, half-crouched shape
awaiting him.

Almost instinctively Shawn dropped into the stance he'd
been taught: arms forward and crooked at the elbows, fists
knotted. Pete's grin widened.

"A real fancy Dan, eh!" he said, and lunged through the
haze.

Starbuck took a slanting step forward, met the rush
with a stiff left, again brought over a hard right. Both
blows landed high on the outlaw's head, had little good re-
sults. Pete, still grinning, turned, moved in, arms churning.

Shawn ignored the obvious attempt at confusing him, feinted left, dodged to the right and suddenly hammered two stinging blows to the man's face.

Brock hesitated, frowned. He appeared puzzled, as if he couldn't understand where the hard-knuckled fists had come from. Shawn watched him narrowly, circled slowly. He slid a glance at Rufe, on his feet, sagged against the wall of the bunkhouse; the man was rubbing at his jaw in a dazed fashion. It was clear he no longer had any interest in the proceedings.

Rutter stood back well out of the way, watching it all with cold, speculative eyes. A bit to his left Tom Gage, hanging onto the reins of the chestnut, was looking on with frank pleasure.

Starbuck, the anger within him now satisfied in pure physical violence, abruptly danced in and flicked Brock on the face with a sliding blow that drew blood. He tapped the outlaw again, lightly, below an eye, brought an immediate welt, followed that with a cross that cracked like a mule skinner's whip when it landed. Pete yelled in rage and lunged forward.

Shawn blocked the charge with an outstretched left, swiftly complemented that with a solid right. Pete halted abruptly, eyes rolling to the back of his head. He caught himself, raised his arms, came on. Again Shawn landed that vicious combination. The other man's knees quivered. His hands dropped heavily to his sides. His head sagged forward, and sinking quietly, he sprawled full length in the dust.

Breathing hard, Starbuck threw a look to Rufe and then to Rutter. Neither seemed inclined to pursue the fight. Stepping back, he recovered his pistol from where it had dropped, thrust it into his waistband. Again touching Rutter and Rufe with his eyes, he crossed to where Brock lay.

Nudging Brock with his toe, he straightened him out to where he was flat on his back. Reaching down, Shawn tripped the tongue of the buckle, and pulled the belt free. Hanging it over his shoulder, he dug into Brock's pockets, drew out a handful of loose coins. Assuming that all belonged to him, he thrust them into his own pocket and turned to face Rutter and Rufe.

"Which one of you slugged me from behind?"

Rutter's eyes narrowed. "You got your goddam belt back—and your money. Don't press your luck—leave it at that."

"Not about to," Starbuck said tightly. "It you?"

The redhaired man shook his head. "Wasn't even there," he murmured.

Shawn's pressing gaze shifted to Rufe. "Leaves you."

"Leaves me," the big man said, and reached for his pistol.

In a single stride Starbuck was on him. With a sweep of his right hand he knocked the weapon to the ground. He caught the man by the arm, swung him half about, smashed a balled fist into his belly. Rufe grunted, doubled over. Instantly a fist thudded into his chin. He straightened up, fell back against the side of the bunkhouse.

From the tail of his eye Shawn saw Rutter drop into a crouch as his hand darted for the pistol on his hip. With a quick, half-turn Starbuck came about, his left hand gripping the forty-five, holding it level on his opponent.

Rutter's fingers had closed about his weapon, stalled. Somewhere a door opened and closed in the heat-filled hush. Starbuck, his gaze never shifting from Rutter, rode out the dragging moments.

"What's it to be?" he asked, finally.

Rutter shrugged, allowed his hand to slide off the butt of his pistol. Shawn relaxed slowly, aware now that there were others in the yard watching besides Tom Gage. A well-dressed man was approaching in short, quick strides. Two of the hired help had paused near a corral, and another, pitchfork across his shoulder, was standing in the doorway of the barn. The faces of two women, one young, were at a window of the main house. . . .

"Supposing you both forget about them irons," the old foreman drawled. "You got some shooting to do, get off the place."

Rutter swung his attention to Gage, raked him with a contemptuous glance, and moved toward Rufe. Starbuck, breathing easier, shook off the tension that gripped him with a stir of his shoulders, crossed to the chestnut. He nodded crisply to the older man.

"Obliged," he said, taking the gelding's leathers. "Didn't aim to start a—"

"Just what the hell's going on here?"

It was the well-dressed man who had apparently come from the main house. He was slim, business-like, somewhere in his forties. He had graying hair and close-set, dark eyes. This would be Sam Underwood.

Gage nodded genially. "Well, Sam, seems that them friends of your'n must've jumped this young fellow, took some of his belongings—that belt he's holding and a bit of cash. He was just getting it back."

The rancher frowned. "You know I don't stand for brawling on my place, Tom—"

"Sure, I know it. But that young rimrocker's sort of all-of-a-sudden-like in his acting. Wasn't nothing I could do about it."

"He a friend of yours?"

"Ain't never seen him before."

Underwood's eyes swept Shawn coolly, appraisingly, and moved on to Rutter and Rufe who were now helping Pete Brock to his feet.

"Mr. Underwood," Shawn said, "my name's Starbuck. Fight was no fault of your foreman's. . . . Rode in to ask—"

The rancher lifted his hand, brushed Shawn aside and moved toward the three defeated men. He pointed to a horse trough near the corrals, and then with a jerk of his head to Rutter, strode across the yard to where a circular bench had been built around the trunk of a large cotton-wood tree.

Starbuck watched the man for a moment, and then drawing his pistol, brushed the dust from it, tested its action. Digging into his saddlebags, he withdrew the holster, slid the belt into the fold, and strapped it about his waist. Dropping the weapon into its leather pocket, he again looked to Gage.

"Sorry about the ruckus. When I rode in had other things on my mind—then I saw them."

"Forget it. Was what I told Sam somewheres close to the truth?"

"Is the truth. Ran into them back in the hills late yesterday. They came at me later in the night—when I was asleep. Rufe—the big one—hit me from behind while I was talking to Brock. Then they robbed me."

"Expect you've cured them of trying that again—on you, anyway," Gage observed drily, and then shook his head. "Seeing you take on all them three at once, put me in mind of a mustang I roped up Montana way—big and strong and feared of nothing—a real rimrocker, he was."

Shawn grinned. "Reckon this is the first time I've ever been called a horse, but I take it you mean it kindly." He glanced toward the bench. Rufe and Pete, both dripping from dousing themselves in the trough, had joined Underwood and Rutter.

"They work here?"

"No, sir!" Gage snapped. "Strangers to me. Rode in a couple hours back, looking for Sam. Friends of his, they claimed, and I guess they are from the way they're talking.

Say—that there was about the fanciest job of cutting a man down to size I ever seen! Where'd you learn to use your fists like that?"

"My pa," Shawn replied, taking the edge of the belt buckle between his fingers and tipping it so the older man could see it better. "He was real good at it. Could have been a champion, I guess if my ma had let him."

"Well, he sure taught you good. Once seen one of them boxing matches. Over in Fort Worth. Black fellow and his manager, touring the country. From England, they was. Picked himself out the biggest man in the saloon and dang nigh beat him to death."

Starbuck nodded. "Pa always said a man's fists could be deadlier than a gun, if they were used right."

"Amen," Gage said. He cocked his head to one side. "Appears to me you've learned how to use both."

Shawn's thick brows pulled together in a frown. "I'm no gunhawk, if that's what you're thinking. But you move around a lot, you learn a lot. Things sort of happen to you and you measure up, or run. Don't like running."

"See what you mean," Gage said thoughtfully. "Just riding through?"

"Not exactly. Was trying to explain that to Mr. Underwood when he walked off. Came here looking for a man —one working for you."

"There's a plenty of them doing that. What's his name?"

Shawn Starbuck grinned wryly, knowing beforehand the reaction he would get when he answered the question. It was an old, familiar procedure.

"I don't rightly know," he said.

◎ 5 ◎

Sam Underwood had been gone when Rutter and the others had arrived. He'd ridden out early that morning to have a look at his south range and, incidentally, to drop by for a few minutes' chat with Greg Cryden who owned the spread below him. Cryden had been in the country for a long time, was well thought of and his influence in political matters was extensive.

Amy Underwood had met Sam at the door when he returned. Her flaccid, colorless features were drawn with concern and there was a troubled look in her eyes. They were her sole claim to beauty, large, dark and soft as those of a deer—and they were the only thing about her that hadn't changed since the day of their marriage.

"They came after you rode off," she had said. "Told me they were old friends of yours from the war. They acted as though I should invite them in, but I didn't like their looks and told them to wait in the bunkhouse. Who are they, Samuel? Something about them gives me the chills."

He had shrugged off her distress, but within him a dread had sprung alive as facets of his past stirred in the shadowy recesses of his mind. Was it Guy Rutter and Brock and Rufe Mysak—and Billy Gault? Three men, Amy had said. Someone was missing. Which one? What did they want?

But he had smiled, assured Amy that everything was all right. It wouldn't do to show alarm in her presence. She never dreamed he could be other than what he had always professed to be—an honest, hard-working, successful rancher well on his way to becoming governor of the Territory.

The same applied to Holly. In the eyes of his stepdaughter, he represented the utmost, a man who could do no wrong—the epitome of what a husband and father should be. To shatter her illusions would break her heart.

Maybe he was upsetting himself over nothing, if, indeed, it was Rutter and the rest of the bunch from the Old Fifth Ohio—and he couldn't be sure of that until he got a look at them. Even if it were them, they could just be riding through, heard he was there, stopped to pass the time of day. Hope rose within him.

"Where'd you send them?" he had asked.

"The bunkhouse," Amy had replied. "I saw them go in."

He had walked to the window, glanced out just in time to see the men coming out of the crew's quarters. His spirits had sagged once more as all the harsh fears lifted again within him, began to claw at his guts.

He had guessed right. Guy Rutter—Pete Brock—Rufe Mysak. All of the bunch who'd been with him that day at Medford's Crossing, all but Billy Gault.

"Do you know them?" Amy had asked.

"Know who?" Holly, entering the room at that moment, had broken in.

"Some men to see your father, honey," Amy had answered. "No one you should meet."

An instant later everything in the yard was in confusion as some stranger, who had been talking to Tom Gage, suddenly tore from his horse and took on Brock and Rufe Mysak, knocking them about like dummies.

Sam Underwood had watched briefly, marveling at the stranger's ability and deriving some enjoyment from the punishment being meted out to Mysak and Brock; and then he had turned away from the window to the door.

"I'll take care of this," he had said in a firm, decisive way, and gone out into the yard to meet the specters from his past.

Now, facing the three men in the cooling shadow of the cottonwood—one he'd hauled in from the river bottom and planted with his own hands ten long years ago—he looked each one over, masking his apprehension with an impersonal smile.

"What brings you men here?"

Rutter's reddish hair was much thinner than it once was, but his small, mean eyes had not changed; the blue was colder, if anything.

"You," Guy Rutter said.

"And I can't say you seem real pleased to see your old army pals again," Mysak, much heavier than in previous years, observed. "Does he, boys?"

Brock, still somewhat dazed, shook his head woodenly. Rutter shrugged, spat.

"All right," Underwood snapped. "I'm glad to see you." And then in an effort to further prove his words, he added, "Where's Gault?"

"Billy? Hell, he's dead," Mysak answered. "Got his fool head shot off in a poker game. About a year after he was mustered out."

"Too bad," Underwood murmured. "Figured you'd all be living back east somewhere. Surprised to see you in this part of the country. Where you headed?"

"Right here," Rutter said in his flat, emotionless way.

The rancher's head lifted in surprise. "You came on purpose to see me? Didn't think anybody—that is—any of the old bunch knew—I—"

"We heard," Rutter said blandly. "Heard all about how you had yourself a big ranch and was doing fine—and how you were in the banking business—was even about to become governor. Told ourselves you'd be real happy to help us with a job we've got in mind."

"Of course. Be happy to do what I can for you," Underwood said, relief in his voice. "Have some influence around the Territory, if I do say so myself. Just what is it you're planning?"

"We're robbing the bank in Las Vegas," Rutter said, and smiled.

Sam Underwood's jaw sagged. "You're *what?*"

"Your hearing's good. Was up in Denver, learned about this bank in Las Vegas—how all the big cattle growers kept their cash in it, same as the army at Fort Union does with its payroll. Sounded real good. We'd been looking for something easy for quite a spell."

"But—you—"

"Sounded even better when we found out one of the owners was an old friend of ours—Sam Underwood."

"Wasn't real sure it was our Sam, not at first anyway," Mysak said. "Then we took us a little trip to Las Vegas and hung around till we got a look at you. Sure enough, it was our Sam—but we was betting it would be all the time. Be like old Sam, we told ourselves, to take his share of that payroll and set himself up in business."

The blood in Underwood's veins had been turning slowly to ice. "That money—share—always intended to send it back, not keep it. . . ."

"But you didn't," Rutter said drily. "Even if you did you got some way of bringing life back into them guards we killed taking it?"

The rancher looked down and shook his head helplessly.

"That was a mistake—a big mistake. I was a fool to throw in with you."

"But you did—and you're coming in with us again or—"

Underwood's eyes, unseeing, were on Pete Brock, now finally recovered and gingerly probing his bruised, discolored face with careful fingers.

"Or—" he prompted halfheartedly.

"This whole country's going to know right quick about the real Sam Underwood—about how he was in on robbing an army paymaster during the war, and how three soldiers got killed trying to stop it."

"But I—"

"How's that going to sound to all those folks who're backing you for governor? How's that fine wife of yours going to take it? Hear she cuts quite a figure with all the high society muckity-mucks in Santa Fe—Denver, even! And you got yourself a daughter who—"

The mention of his family stiffened Sam Underwood. His features hardened and a sternness came into his eyes.

"You'll find it won't be so easy—not with me—"

"Oh, it'll be easy, all right," Rutter cut in. "About the easiest thing a man could imagine. We just haven't worked this deal up overnight, Sam. We've been planning it out for better'n a month."

"Ever since we run out of cash," Pete Brock volunteered.

"Last little job we done over Kansas way didn't pay off so good," Mysak added.

Guy Rutter waited in sullen patience for the two men to speak, and then again turned to Underwood.

"We got a good look at your bank, know just how to handle it. Vault ain't much. Rufe can blow it with no problems. And if you're getting an idea about tipping off the sheriff or somebody, you better forget it damn quick."

"You don't think—"

"That part's all covered, too. We brought us a lady friend who's sort of been running with us the last couple of years. She got herself a job in that Gold Dollar Saloon in Las Vegas. She's keeping a letter for us."

Underwood said, "A letter?"

"A real important one. It's made out to the U.S. Marshal, and it tells all about that payroll robbery and killing at Medford's Crossing. Gives all our names. I even dug up some of the newspaper stories about it, put them in the envelope. If anything happens to us while we're cleaning

33

out your bank—or after—she hands that letter over to the first lawman she can get to."

The rancher's features had drained of all color. "Then she knows—"

"All she knows is what she's to do with the envelope if you double-cross us."

"Guy's fixed things up plenty good," Mysak said. "Guess you can see that, so it's up to you to make sure everything goes off all right."

Underwood mopped at the sweat covering his face. "But—I'm half owner of that bank. Some of the money in it is mine—"

Rutter shrugged. "Make you feel any better, we'll give you a little cut of what we get. Maybe it'll be enough to cover your losses."

The rancher wagged his head. "No—I won't touch it! I'm not going through again what I did after that payroll robbery—and killing."

"Up to you. But you figure yourself in, clean up to the collarbone. Now, first thing we want is a key to the back door of that bank building. Never mind the safe. Rufe'll take care of it. And we want a place to hang out. Just won't be smart for us to lay around the town for the next couple of days. Somebody might get nosy."

"You can hire us on as cowhands," Mysak suggested. "We'll make real good ones—doing nothing."

Rutter nodded. "Gives us an alibi, too, in case somebody gets lucky and sees us coming out of the bank. Be up to you to speak up and say it couldn't have been us because we work for you, and we were all here together on the ranch the night of the robbery. Nobody will dispute the word of Sam Underwood."

"I can't do it," the rancher mumbled uncertainly. "I can't get mixed up—"

"You're already mixed up in it," Guy Rutter snarled. "Don't you forget that—not for a minute! Now, if you don't want your share of the cash we'll be taking, all right. Makes more for us. Thing is—just don't get in our way and be goddamned sure you do what you're told and that you keep your mouth shut."

"Yessir," Mysak said. "You don't, everything's going to blow right up in your face—and the next thing you know you'll be peeking through the bars of a cell in the Federal pen!"

"But—I—well, I've got to think—"

"Think—nothing!" Rutter snapped. "You've got that

34

done for you. You're in this deal whether you like it or not."

"And since we're working for you and we're all flat busted," Pete Brock said, managing a grin, "we'll take a little of our wages ahead of time. Maybe fifty apiece."

"Now, that's a smart idea!" Mysak exclaimed, rubbing his big hands together. "I recollect a little yellow-haired gal back there in the Gold Dollar that I got me some unfinished business with. . . . Supposing you make that a even hundred dollars a piece, Sam."

Underwood's shoulders settled into a helpless slump. "Don't carry that kind of money on me."

"But I'm betting a big man like you'll easy have that much in the house—maybe in a tin box or a safe. You want us to have a look?"

"I'll get it," the rancher said heavily.

"Make it a hundred flat, like Rufe said." Rutter's words came as an order, uncompromising.

Underwood nodded, started to turn away when Rutter caught him by the arm.

"Better tell that foreman of yours about us working for you. He don't cotton to us much."

"I'll tell him," the rancher said, "but if you're planning on hanging around here, you'd better play it smart and get along with him."

◎ 6 ◎

Tom Gage pulled off his hat and rubbed at his balding head while a puzzled expression covered his weather-seamed face.

"That sure does kind of put us in a fix, don't it?" he drawled. "You're a-looking for somebody but you don't know who."

"Guess that's the way it sounds," Shawn replied with a smile. "Fact is, it's my brother Ben. . . . Ben Starbuck. Pretty sure he's not using that name nowadays."

The old foreman pursed his lips. "I see. . . . What's he look like?"

"Can't tell you much about that either. Been ten years since I last saw him—and I was just a kid. Likely he'll be dark, on the stocky side. He had blue eyes."

"You sure don't give a man much to go on," Gage murmured.

"Only thing I know for sure is he's got a scar just above the left eye. Only about an inch long and it's kind of hard to notice."

Tom Gage studied his gnarled hands. "Just don't right off recollect anybody around here with a mark like that. Somebody say we had a man who did?"

"Ran into a cattle buyer up Kansas way. Was asking for Ben. He said your trail boss sort of fit the description."

"Henry Smith?"

"Buyer didn't know his name, only that he bossed Underwood's trail drives—and been doing it last three or four years."

"That's Henry, all right. It's where he's at right now. . . . Come to think on it, he does kind of match up to the man you're looking for. Don't remember the scar, though."

"You'd have to look close for it. He got it when we

36

were kids playing in the rocks back of the farm. You say he's on a drive now?"

"Drive's over. Likely on his way back. Ought to be showing up next day or two."

Shawn glanced at the four men gathered under the cottonwood. The rancher appeared strained, upset. Rutter and the two others were half smiling, joking in a smug sort of way.

"Hate to hear that," he said, touching his jaw with a fingertip. Pete Brock had got in one good blow during the fight, and the spot was tender. "Was hoping I could find out one way or another today—know if I'd made another long ride for nothing."

"It real important you find him, that it?"

Starbuck nodded. "Guess I could ride on to Las Vegas, put up there a couple of days, then drop back. How far is it?"

"Half a day—less if you get right along. But there ain't no sense in your doing that. Henry'll be here tomorrow most likely—for sure the next day—all depending on how drunk him and the rest of the drovers get after the settling-up's done. You can wait here."

Shawn ducked his head at Underwood. "What about *him?* Don't think he's going to feel very kindly toward me after the ruckus I had with his friends."

Gage shrugged. "You know what, I ain't so sure they're all that much friends. But don't let it bother you none—Sam, I mean. He leaves running this ranch up to me, him being busy politicking and banking and squiring his missus around to all the high-toned shindigs going on."

"I understand. It'd be a favor if you'd let me pull off in those trees back of the corrals, set myself up a camp there, and wait—"

"I'm damned if you'll do any such thing!" Gage snapped indignantly. "Long as I'm around any decent man's welcome to stop over, stick his legs under the crew's vittle table, and use an empty bunk. Been that way since I can recollect, and I ain't about to let it change."

Starbuck smiled. "Appreciate that—and I'll be glad to lend a hand. Worked cows and horses aplenty, all over the country. And I'm not above doing yard chores."

"Help's something we sure don't need. Sam's maybe kind of got big ideas for hisself, but he's square when it comes to dealing with the hired hands. Never lays a man off when things get slack the way most ranchers do. Just keeps them on, paying regular wages every month."

"Shows it," Shawn said, glancing around. "Can see the

37

men take pride in the place and keep it looking fine. One way of them saying thanks, I guess."

"There's them that likes to stay busy doing things," Gage said drily, "and there's them that don't."

"Man's lucky to ride for an outfit like this."

The old foreman stroked his moustache. "Cows is cows. Makes no difference what kind of a place they're on, they're still plain ornery, mean, cantankerous critters that can drive a man to plucking out his eyeballs. But there ain't no sense us standing here in the hot sun jawing. Expect you'd like to wash off some of that dust, and then—"

"Tom—"

Gage turned, faced Underwood who was approaching with his friends trailing slightly behind.

"I'm hiring these men."

"Hiring—to do what?"

"Whatever you can figure out for them," Underwood snapped, nettled at the foreman's belligerence. "Names are Guy Rutter, Pete Brock, and Rufe Mysak. We were in the war together."

"So they was telling me. . . . Hell, Sam, hired help's so thick around here now you can't stir them with a stick—"

"Realize that, but I want them put on anyway. They can do range riding."

"We're real good at doing that," Mysak said with a broad wink at Pete Brock.

Gage sighed resignedly. "All right, Sam, it's your money. I'll fix them up."

Starbuck, waiting off to one side, felt the rancher's eyes upon him.

"You waiting to see me?"

"Waiting to see Hank Smith," the foreman replied before Shawn could answer. "I'm inviting him to bunk in with me."

The rancher studied Starbuck speculatively. "You an old friend of Hank's?"

"Maybe. Not sure yet."

Underwood looked puzzled, then shrugged, said, "You're mighty fancy with those fists of yours. . . . That gun, too. It your line of work?"

"Cowhand, mostly," Shawn said.

"I see," the rancher murmured, and turning, strode for the house.

Starbuck watched him briefly, and then, arms folded across his chest, faced Rutter and his two shadows. All were considering him intently.

"We take things up where we left off?" he asked in a quiet voice.

Guy Rutter's features hardened fleetingly, and then he produced a forced smile. "All forgot, far as I'm concerned. Same with you boys?" he added, glancing to Brock and Mysak.

Rufe nodded. Pete Brock made no answer, but continued to stare sullenly at Shawn. Rutter's small eyes glittered.

"What about it, Pete?"

"I ain't making no promises," Brock answered. "I figure I got me a few good licks coming."

"Any time you say," Starbuck countered. "Everything's settled and I'm holding no grudge. Got my stuff back. That's the main thing I was interested in."

"And you'll forget it, too, Pete!" Rutter snapped. "Told you we didn't have no time to be messing around with a penny-ante thing like that belt. Forget it, hear? We can't afford—"

Guy Rutter's words ended abruptly. He looked away as if regretting what he had said, and then, after a moment, came back to Tom Gage.

"All right, Grandpa, where you want us to put up?"

The foreman bristled. "My name ain't grandpa—it's Tom Gage—and you can roost with the crows far as I'm concerned. But Sam said I was to take you on, so I reckon that mean's you'll bed down with the crew."

"In there?" Rutter asked, thumbing at the bunkhouse.

Gage nodded. "In there. You'll find some extra bunks. Pick some."

Guy Rutter turned away. "Pity we ain't friends of yours instead of the man that owns the place, then maybe we could have a special place to stay."

The foreman grinned maliciously. "Yeh, a real pity, ain't it?"

Brock and Rufe Mysak wheeled to follow Rutter. Pete glanced back over his shoulder. "Grandpa, you be sure and call us when supper's ready, hear?"

"I ain't calling nobody. When grub's ready, the cook'll hammer on his bar. If you don't come, then go without."

"Sure don't want that to happen," Mysak said, shaking his head. "Boys, we'd better keep our ears open."

Gage watched them until they had reached the crew's quarters and entered and then looked at Shawn. "If them three are what Sam calls his friends, I figure he's a lot better off with his enemies."

"Could cause you a lot of worry," Starbuck admitted. "Don't let them get under your hide."

"Well, Sam or no Sam, I don't aim to take no sass off them. . . . Now, what I was about to say—you're wanting to clean up a mite—"

"Horse trough will do me fine."

"Horse trough, hell! There's a sink and a pump in my cabin. Use it. Bring your gear along, too, since you'll be bunking with me."

Restless, unable to sleep despite his weariness, Starbuck sat up, swung his legs over the side of the bed. An arm's length away, Tom Gage snored in deep cadence. He guessed it was because Henry Smith could be Ben that he was finding it difficult to settle down. But it was always like that—the waiting, the not knowing, was hard.

Slipping into pants and boots, he rose, crossed to the door and stepped out into the cool night. One window showed light in the main house; over everything lay a heavy silence. The smell of sage was strong in the air and far off a coyote gave voice to his loneliness.

Almost at once an ease began to fill Shawn Starbuck, release the tautness, soothe the raw ends of his nerves. A serene patience came over him bringing contentment.

Maybe this was where the search would end—here on Sam Underwood's ranch. Gage had seemed to think Henry Smith fit what little description he had given of his brother; and there was the fact that the name—Henry Smith—in itself, didn't exactly ring true. Men, wishing to hide their real identities, usually adopted the simplest, most commonplace designation they could think of.

It was as good as any lead he'd had yet, Shawn thought as he strolled toward the corral into which he'd turned the chestnut. The cattle buyer and Tom Gage had both given him cause for hope.

He halted, suddenly aware of three figures standing in the half dark to his left. Rufe Mysak's voice came to him.

"Doing some spying on us, cowboy?"

Starbuck's muscles tightened. He hadn't expected to meet anyone at that hour of the night, much less these three.

"Getting some air," he replied.

Rutter's comment was dry. "Sure, and you just happened to come after that air on this side of the yard."

The solitary light in the main house blinked out. The thought came to Shawn that Rutter and the others had been visiting with Underwood. Probably hashing over old times in the army. He failed to understand what difference it made whether he had seen them or not. Spying?

Vaguely irked, he said, "Suit yourself. That's the way it is."

"I've got a hunch," Rutter continued in that same, level voice, "that you're going to step out in front of us once too often. Might be a real smart thing for you to get your belongings, saddle up, and ride on—now."

Starbuck came about slowly until his back was against the pole bars of the corral. He'd been a fool to come out without his gun, but then he doubted if they'd try using theirs. . . . And if it came to fists again. . . .

"Best you overlook that hunch," he said. "Happens I'm not ready to pull out. Expect I'll be around a couple a days or so—more if need be. After I've done what I came for, I'll move on."

"Could be we'll do a little persuading," Mysak said insinuatingly. "Now, Pete here feels he's got a call coming. Was we to step in, give him a hand—"

"And raise the whole damned place!" Rutter finished in disgust. "Show some sense, Rufe."

"Then let's herd him off into the brush," Brock said eagerly. "He ain't packing no gun—and nobody'll hear."

"Then what? Comes daylight and somebody finds him—"

"What difference that make?"

"Plenty, goddammit! Get it in your head—we don't want to stir up trouble around here. Draw too much attention. We'll leave it up to him—give him till noon tomorrow. If he ain't gone by then, well, there's plenty of open country we can bank on. You savvy what I'm driving at, Starbuck?"

"Plain enough," Shawn answered. "Only it doesn't mean anything. I'll pull out when I'm ready—and that'll be after I've had a talk with the man I'm waiting for."

"I ain't buying that," Rutter said flatly.

Mysak's bulk shifted in the shadows as he turned to face the redhead. "You mean he ain't hunting for no brother, like he claims?"

"Just what I mean. I figure that's a lot of bull, a way to hide what he really is."

Brock said, "What's that?"

"Let him tell you," Rutter replied. "Talk up, Starbuck. You ain't no plain cow-nurse. You don't act like it and you don't look like it. I'd say you was a *lawman* of some kind."

Shawn smiled into the darkness. "Done a lot of things

41

moving round, looking for my brother. Never happened to take on a lawman's job, though."

"More'n likely he's some kind of hired gun," Mysak said.

"Wrong again."

A silence followed that, broken finally when Rutter said, "Anyway, can't see as it matters none, one way or other. You got till noon tomorrow to haul freight, mister. If you're still around then—well, you'd best start watching your back trail."

"I'll be here," Starbuck said in a soft voice, "unless I've finished with my business."

"Take my advice," Rutter said. "Be finished."

◎ 7 ◎

Starbuck said nothing to Tom Gage about his encounter with Rutter and his friends that next morning. The foreman was riled enough at being forced to add them to his already overloaded crew, and Shawn could see where little could be gained.

As far as Rutter's threats went, they meant nothing to him. He would stay, as he had declared, until Henry Smith returned and he was satisfied that the trail boss was or was not Ben.

At the crew table in a room off the kitchen for the early meal, he sat next to Gage, acknowledged the introductions the older man felt inclined to make, and paid no attention to Guy Rutter, Brock, or Mysak who sat on the opposite side of the long counter. Gage introduced them also to the hands present grudgingly, and only out of necessity. As on most ranches, strangers riding across the open range were always suspect and required to identify themselves. It wouldn't do to have Sam Underwood's three army chums roped and ridden off the land by punchers bent only on doing their duty.

Rutter finished the meal before Brock and Rufe. Rising, he sauntered over to where Gage and Starbuck were dawdling over a last cup of coffee. Most of the men had already moved on and were in the yard mounting up and heading out in the early morning light to assume their various jobs.

"You got something special for us to do?" Rutter asked, picking at his teeth.

Gage twisted half about on his chair. "Sure have. There's a brake—four, maybe five miles south of here. Some of the boys are down there chasing strays out of the brush. Go down and give them a hand."

Brock and Mysak, finally through with their plates also, rose and moved to Rutter's side. Brock assumed a pained expression, and said, "Now, that sounds like real hard work! I don't calculate old Sam figured on us doing something like that."

Mysak grinned his wide, toothy grin. "Not us, no sir. We're mighty close friends of his'n."

"I don't give a hoot in hell who you are!" Gage roared, eyes blazing. "That's what I'm telling you to do, and if you don't aim—"

"What's the trouble here?" Underwood's voice came from the doorway.

Gage jumped to his feet. "These here hands you hired—"

"Never mind, Tom," the rancher cut in soothingly. "I'll see to them myself." He hesitated and a forced smile came to his lips. "Don't mind them, now. They always were great ones for joshing a man."

The old foreman stood in silence. Rutter and Brock wheeled, swaggered toward the waiting Underwood. Mysak nodded, said, "Sure, don't you mind us none," and followed his friends and the rancher into the yard.

Gage, his face flushed to a bright red, swore deeply. "If that's the way Sam Underwood wants this here ranch run, then, by damn, he can run it hisself," he said, and started for the door.

Starbuck caught him by the arm. "Don't fly off the handle," he murmured. "Just what they're trying to do—get your goat. Let it ride. Underwood acts to me like a man who's got himself some trouble. Worst favor you could do him is quit now."

The foreman relented, his gaze on the four men swinging to the saddle. After a moment he wheeled.

"You know something I don't?"

Starbuck downed the last of his coffee, rose to his feet. "Nope, only that it's not hard to spot a man who's got a cougar by the tail."

Gage nodded slowly. "Kind of got that idea about Sam myself. Ain't never seen him act like this."

"It'll blow over. Everything always does. . . . You want me to ride down, help with those strays in the brake?"

"Hell no, I don't!" Gage barked testily. "Was sending them there just to rid myself of them, not because I was needing them. . . . You do what you please. Maybe I can think up a chore or two later."

"Sing out when you do," Starbuck said. "Like to pay for my keep. I'll be at the corral. Think I'll rub down my horse. Haven't given him a good going over in quite a spell."

The foreman bobbed his head. "Get anything you need

from Manuel, in the stable. He looks after the boss's horses. Be seeing you later. There's a few things I got to do."

Shawn moved into the yard with Gage, turned off to the corral where he had put the chestnut. Slipping a halter on the big gelding, he led him to a hitchrack near the barn, sought out the hostler, and obtained a steel comb and a stiff brush.

The gelding was still a bit shaggy from his winter coat, and there was considerable mud caked on his shanks and fetlocks, accumulated during their passage along the several creeks they'd encountered. His tail also nested more than a fair share of cockleburs.

Shawn set to work and kept at it steadily for better than an hour. Soon the chestnut began to take on a new look; his reddish coat glowed sleekly in the sunlight while his white-stockinged legs became trim and clean. However, the burrs were hard to pick out. Many were deeply entwined in the coarse hair and Starbuck worked at them diligently, not wanting to cut away any more of the black strands than necessary, but knowing the troublesome burrs had to be removed.

"You're going to a lot of bother. . . ."

At the sound of the voice Shawn looked up. A girl of perhaps seventeen or eighteen, blond, with dark brown eyes, was standing at the end of the rack. She was nicely shaped and dressed in a white shirtwaist, corduroy riding skirt and soft, black boots. A bright blue scarf was around her head.

Starbuck grinned. "If I don't get them out he'll be mad at me all the rest of summer."

The girl laughed, moved closer. "I'm Holly Underwood. Are you going to work for my father?"

Shawn shook his head. "Just passing through. Stopped by to see a fellow."

"Oh—a drifter," she murmured, a thread of scorn underlying her tone.

"Not exactly," Starbuck replied, his own voice somewhat stiff.

Holly took an impulsive step toward him. "Oh, I don't mean anything bad by that! It's only—well—I think a man should be like my father—settle down, work hard, make something big of his life. You can't do that wandering around, going nowhere—doing nothing. . . . Can I help?"

Without waiting for him to answer, she grasped a thick

45

strand of the chestnut's tail in her hands and began to pick at the burrs.

"Not always easy for a man to be like your pa—father."

She nodded, said frankly, "He's different from most men. Real smart. A fine person—good to everybody." Holly broke off, smiled disarmingly. "I don't mean that you're not, Mr.—"

"Starbuck. Shawn's my first name—without the mister."

"All right, Shawn. I—I'm sorry for how I said that. I guess my father means so much to me that I'm always comparing him to other men without thinking." She glanced toward the barn, called, "Manuel—will you get my horse, please?"

Starbuck worked out the last of the burrs.

"He's certainly a beautiful horse," the girl said admiringly. "How old is he?"

"Around four. We've covered a lot of territory together. Never let me down yet."

"That's because you take good care of him," she said approvingly. "I like that. Show's you're not one of the ordinary cowhand kind."

"Reason for that maybe. Man puts in a full day's work on the range, he doesn't feel much like playing nursemaid to a horse when he comes in."

She was studying him closely. "You don't talk like a cowhand, either."

"My mother was a schoolteacher. Took a lot of pains to see that I got some teaching. Guess a little of it stuck."

Holly glanced to the barn. The hostler was leading out a tall sorrel. "I'm going for a ride," she said. "Why don't you come along? I could show you some of the ranch, that is—if you've nothing better to do."

He had nothing better to do, Shawn decided quickly. "Be my pleasure. Just give me time to saddle up and we'll be on our way."

◎ 8 ◎

They rode south out of the yard, meeting Tom Gage a short distance from the ranch buildings. The foreman smiled, raised his hand in salutation, but did not stop.

"It's a fine place," Shawn said some time later when they had topped a small rise and were looking out onto a vast, rolling plain green with grass.

"Seventy thousand acres," Holly said proudly. "Most of it just like that. There's no better ranch in the whole Territory."

"Man would have no trouble raising prime beef here," Starbuck admitted, and then pointed to a distant mound of dark earth and rock. "What's that?"

"An old Indian ruin. I used to go there a lot before I went away. I'd dig for arrowheads, things like that."

"Away? Where?"

"Only to Santa Fe. I attended the Academy there. Graduated last year. . . . I sort of had ideas about being a schoolteacher, too—like your mother."

"But you changed your mind."

"Yes—or maybe it was my father. He didn't think it would be exactly proper for me to work." Holly paused, smiled, looked squarely at Shawn. "I guess I've said the wrong thing again."

Starbuck shrugged. "Nothing wrong in that—or in your wanting to be a schoolmarm, either, far as I can see. But I reckon I know how your pa felt. Man in his position—guess it wouldn't be right for his daughter to work."

"That's the way he put it. I suppose it didn't really matter to me—and I certainly didn't want to embarrass him. Especially if he does become governor."

"The chances pretty good for that?"

"He says they are, and he's usually right. He's well known, being half owner of the bank in Vegas, and President of the Cattleman's Association, and all that."

"Expect he'll make it then," Shawn said, touching the chestnut lightly with his spurs. "Let's take a closer look at your Indian ruin."

They rode off the rise at an easy lope, reached the flat and drew the horses down to a walk. Starbuck felt Holly's eyes upon him and he turned to her questioningly.

"Something's wrong?"

"I was thinking about your mother. . . . What was she like?"

"I was pretty much a kid when she died. I can remember she was tall, had a quiet way of speaking. Could be firm when she wanted to be, though. My pa always said I favored her—had the same eyes and looks while Ben, my brother, took after him. . . . Always wished she'd lived a little longer. Things probably would have been different."

"It was different with me," Holly said, her gaze fixed on the still distant ruin. "My father isn't my real father, you know."

Shawn shook his head. "No, I didn't know."

"My real father was killed in the war. Mother and I moved out here after his death—there was nothing left of the family plantation in Virginia—to live with some old friends."

"And that's where he met your mother?"

Holly nodded. "He was just getting his ranch started. He'd come to see Mr. Cameron who owns the bank—they're the friends we came to live with—about buying up some property. Mr. Cameron brought him home to supper that night. Mother and he were married a month later. . . . He was good to us. Everything has turned out so well."

"A fine thing for everybody all around."

"My own father couldn't have done more for me," Holly said. "Where do you come from, Shawn? Your original home, I mean."

"Farm up in the Muskingum country of Ohio. It was sold when my pa died."

"And you've been wandering ever since?"

"Ever since." He could see no reason to tell her of Ben, although he was finding conversation and being with her very pleasant.

"Where will you go when you leave here?"

"North, I reckon. Want to take a look at Colorado. Then head on up into Wyoming, maybe Montana."

"You could stay here," she said impulsively. "I think my father likes you—and you said yourself that we have a fine ranch."

48

It would be wonderful to settle down and—he had to admit it—be near Holly Underwood. But that was not possible, unless his search for Ben came to an end with his meeting of Henry Smith. However, he could not make plans of any sort; that was a fact of life he'd learned to accept long ago. One day, perhaps—and if Henry Smith did prove to be Ben, then—

"Be fine," he said noncommittally.

"I'd like it, too, Shawn," Holly said and then quickly added, "That's a strange name. Does it have some special meaning?"

"Indian. Short for Shawnee. Ma gave it to me. She once taught some Shawnee children. Took a fancy to it, I guess."

"I like the sound of it. . . . She must have been a wonderful person. What was your father like?"

A recollection of Hiram Starbuck rolled through Shawn's mind, and unconsciously a stiffness crept into his tone. "He was a good man. Maybe a bit on the rough side, but you had to be that way back in those days when he was getting started. . . . Learned a lot from him—mostly how to look after myself."

Holly's face brightened at once. "Did he teach you to fight the way you were doing yesterday? Father said you were a boxer."

He looked at her in surprise, then recalled the faces he'd seen in the ranch-house window. "Too bad you had to see that."

"I've seen men fight before," Holly said. "In Sante Fe —even here on the ranch when nobody knew I was around. I never saw anyone fight the way you did."

"Pa was very good at it. Used to give exhibitions every Saturday back in Ohio. Men would drive in for miles just to see him put on a match."

Holly sighed heavily. "You have the most interesting family—and life. I have—well, hardly anything."

"Only a father who's probably one of the biggest and most important men in the Territory of New Mexico," Shawn said with a smile. "And on top of that—everything you want."

"That's still nothing when you come right down to it. For me, personally, I mean. Oh, I love the parties and the balls in Santa Fe and Vegas, and things like that, but I still—"

She let it hang there. Shawn gave her a sidelong glance, did not press her for a further explanation. It was best to not get involved in such matters—and besides, if she wanted to unload her troubles on him, it would be not at his insistence. Holly, however, didn't realize how fortunate she was. He supposed that was normal. Most persons seemed never to understand how well off they were until something changed and it was too late to go back.

The crumbled walls of the pueblo were just ahead. Reaching the first scatter of rock and round-edged mud bricks, they slowly circled the perimeter, cut finally onto a narrow, beaten trail and made their way to the highest point. A few, half-buried wall remnants still remained to form the outline of separate rooms. There were signs of digging here and there. Shawn pointed to the nearest.

"You, or the prairie dogs?"

Holly laughed, swung off her sorrel. "Me. I spent a lot of time here—once."

Shawn guided his horse to the top ledge, a point where redskinned sentinels had, no doubt, centuries ago maintained watch for hostile invaders.

Abruptly he halted. Four riders had pulled up in the shade of a small tree in a coulee a hundred yards or so distant. He recognized Sam Underwood instantly. And then, one by one, he picked out Guy Rutter, Mysak, and Pete Brock.

They appeared to be discussing something important, with Underwood slightly apart facing his friends and using his hands to emphasize his words. The three men were merely staring at him, listening. Finally Rutter shook his head, and motioning to Brock and Mysak, wheeled about and moved off toward the definite scar of a road that ran on into the west.

"We should get back . . ."

Starbuck turned at once and swung the gelding back down the incline to where the girl was scuffing about with the toe of her boot.

"Expect so," he said glancing at the sun. "Must be getting close to dinner time."

His mind was not on what he was saying, was instead mulling over the angry scene he had just witnessed. No doubt an argument had been in progress—one Rutter and the others had won simply by riding off.

He started to mention the nearby presence of her father to Holly, thought better of it. If there was something wrong between Sam Underwood and his one-time fellow soldiers, it would be better to let him handle it. Setting the girl to worrying over the father she worshipped would be pointless.

He watched her mount, and then followed her down the

50

trail to the flat where they cut north, heading for the long rise beyond which lay the ranch.

Holly was quiet on the return trip, holding her horse to a steady jog that allowed small opportunity for conversation. That she had something weighty on her mind was evident, however, and when they reached the ridge and were moving toward the bottom of the slope that ended near the ranch house, she suddenly faced Shawn.

"I—I meant what I said about you staying here. I'd like it very much, Shawn."

He started to voice his regret, cushion his refusal with an explanation as to why that was impossible, but the girl veered away from him sharply, and spurring her long-legged sorrel, raced for the yard, giving him no chance to speak.

He watched her go, his thoughts suddenly dark and heavy. She couldn't realize how much he would like to stay, should Sam Underwood make him an offer; but it was out of the question unless Henry Smith—

Starbuck cast that from his mind. Too many times hope had risen, only to be dashed to earth again when a man he felt certain would be Ben was not. He'd learned not to allow such hope to arise—only to wait and see. . . . And never make far-reaching plans for the future.

Turning his horse into the yard, he angled toward the corral, seeing Manuel leading Holly's sorrel into the barn as he crossed over. She was already inside the house, he supposed.

Halting, he stepped down, and immediately began to pull his gear from the chestnut. He heard the hard thud of boot heels behind him, and then Tom Gage's voice.

"Have yourself a ride?"

Shawn nodded. "Went over to those Indian ruins."

The foreman nodded and said, "The little gal used to spend a lot of time there, digging about. Many's the time I had to go scouting after her for her ma. Reckon she had a kind of feeling for the place. Told me once—she weren't no more'n a little button then, six maybe seven—the only friends she had was the people who used to live in that old pueblo. . . . Seems to have took quite a shine to you."

"Expect she's curious, mostly. Same way folks like to look at a two-headed calf," Starbuck said, throwing his gear over the top bar of the corral.

Gage cocked his head to one side. "Maybe."

"Anyway," Shawn said quietly, "that's all it had better be. . . . Underwood come in yet?"

"Rode in a few minutes ahead of you two. Said he'd put

51

his friends to work on the north range. Set them to drifting some stock over onto new grass."

Starbuck stared off across the low hills. When he had seen the rancher he was well south of the ranch—not north. And Rutter and the others certainly were not engaged in moving cattle. Again he reminded himself that it was no business of his, but he did voice one question.

"That road near the ruins. Looks fairly well traveled. Where's it go?"

"Las Vegas. It's the main one. Cuts across Sam's land from the east. . . . Come on, best we grab ourselves a bite to eat before the cook gets all worked up."

◎ 9 ◎

The afternoon passed and Henry Smith put in no appearance. Shawn whiled away the hours helping Manuel, the hostler, in the stable, working with Sam Underwood's prize horses, currying, brushing them vigorously, cleaning their hooves and generally performing all the small tasks he took pleasure in.

The rancher had a fine string of horses for the personal use of himself and his family: a matched team of whites to draw a gleaming black surrey, Holly's sorrel, a bay for his own use, and another white that was Mrs. Underwood's but which she now, according to Manuel, seldom rode.

Shawn had an easy, natural way with animals, and he enjoyed working with them. When darkness came and the cook announced the evening meal with a loud clanging on an iron bar hanging just outside the kitchen door, Underwood's riding and driving stock never looked in better condition.

"If you can spare yourself," Tom Gage said from the doorway of the barn, "it's time to be eating again."

Starbuck grinned, washed up and went to the crew's dining quarters with the foreman. When they had seated themselves at the long table, Gage glanced around and shrugged.

"Them friends of Sam's ain't showed up yet. Was they around this afternoon while I was gone?"

Shawn said, "Didn't see them. Was in the barn most of the time, though."

He could have gone further into the matter, told how he had seen Rutter, with Brock and Mysak, riding west on the Las Vegas road after their meeting with Underwood, but again he felt it was no business of his and so remained silent. If Gage pressed the subject, however, he would be forced to tell. He owed that much to the old man.

But he'd drop it there, not bother him with an accounting of his meeting with the three men that previous night, and a report of the ultimatum Guy Rutter had issued. He had decided that before and he'd stick with it. His problems were his own. If Rutter intended to make something of his presence at Underwood's when they came face to face again, he'd handle it himself. Tom Gage had enough worries.

"*Senor*...."

Starbuck, roused from his thoughts, turned to see a small Mexican boy at his elbow.

"The *patron* is send me to say he would talk with you." A smile parted the young, dark face as he swung then to Gage. "You will also come, *Senor Caporal.*"

Tom squeezed the boy's arm affectionately. "All right, Juanito. We'll be there's soon as we're done."

The youngster trotted off, disappearing into a hallway that apparently led deeper into the main house. Gage studied his coffee.

"Now, I wonder what Sam's got squirming around in his mind?"

Starbuck grinned, resumed his meal. "Maybe he doesn't like drifters going riding with his daughter."

"Could be," the foreman replied laconically.

When they had finished, Gage led the way—not through the corridor, but out into the yard and along a path that circled to the front of the house.

"Sam's missus don't allow the hired hands to go traipsing across her carpets no more," he explained. "Was a time when it was fine with her, but since they got to be such biggity folks, we ain't welcome inside. Sam's even built hisself a office at the end of the front porch. That's close as we can get to being under his roof. Amy Underwood's a fine woman but she's sure changed."

"You've worked for Sam a long time?" Starbuck asked as they rounded the end of the structure and stepped up onto the wide gallery.

"Since he bought the place from Jud Higgins—right after he hit this country. Might say I sort of come with the land. Was Jud's foreman, too."

Underwood was seated behind a massive, carved desk when they entered his business quarters. It was a fairly large room and several lithographs and calendars hung on the walls in the company of the mounted head of a large mule deer. No carpet covered the floor but there were half a dozen or so comfortable cowhide chairs arranged to face the desk.

"Wanted to tell you," Gage began before he was even seated, "them three yahoos you hired never showed up for supper. You reckon they've gone and got themselves lost?"

The rancher stirred, laid aside the sheaf of papers through which he was leafing. "Guess I forgot to mention it. Told them they could ride in to Vegas after they got that stock moved. Seems they felt like blowing off a little steam."

"Damn it, Sam!" Gage exploded irritably. "You ought to tell a man when you do something like that. Can't run a ranch with two of us giving orders."

Starbuck listened, surprised at Underwood's words. It had appeared from the hill that Rutter and the two men with him had made their own decision about visiting Las Vegas. And there was the additional fact that they had not been working, were far from the north range. Why would the rancher lie to his own foreman?

"Understand from my daughter, Starbuck, that you're sort of taken with my place."

Shawn became aware that the rancher was speaking to him. He nodded. "It's a fine ranch, Mr. Underwood."

"Call me Sam, same as everybody else. It took a lot of hard work to build it up—on my part and Tom's, too. Owe him plenty."

Some of the anger faded from the old foreman's eyes. "Reckon we can stack the Sunrise brand up against the best of them seven days a week," he said. "There something you wanted to talk about?"

Underwood opened a desk drawer and withdrew a box of cigars. He offered the container to Gage who selected one, eyed it appreciatively. Shawn declined. When he did smoke, which wasn't often, he preferred a cigarette. The rancher chose a cigar for himself, settled back.

"Had it in mind to offer Starbuck a job," he said. "Being my foreman, I naturally wanted you to set in on the talking."

"Doing what?" Gage asked, frowning. "Sure'd like to have him around but we've got more cowhands than cows now, seems like."

"Wasn't exactly thinking of him as a cowhand."

Gage's frown deepened. He bit off the end of his stogie, searched about for a match. Shawn, mulling the rancher's words through his mind, glanced out the window. Evidently Holly had used her persuasive powers on her father. He guessed he could use a job for a while but he wasn't so sure it would be wise to accept one from Underwood—not with the girl around.

"Then what—"

The rancher leaned forward, features intent. "You know how things are shaping up for me, Tom. All this talk of the governor's chair, and there's a good chance I'll be buying Ira Cameron out at the bank, taking over the whole shebang as sole owner."

"Figured it'd come to that someday. Ira's getting a mite old."

"Means I've got to do a lot of running around and such. I need a good man—one I can trust to sort of be, well, my right hand. Like you are here on the ranch. I leave the running of it to you and never worry about it. Now I need the same sort of man to go with me—"

"A hired gun?" Starbuck asked quietly.

The rancher studied the still unlit end of his smoke. "I suppose you might put it that way—but you'd be more of my assistant. You'd have jobs to do, errands to run. Important at times that I get a message to certain men, maybe in Vegas, or maybe in Santa Fe. Sending it by stagecoach mail is too slow. You'd carry it personally. Be a hell of a lot faster and I'd know for sure it was getting delivered to the right party.

"I suppose there'd be some bodyguarding to it. Tom can tell you there's times when I'm carrying quite a bit of money on me—times I'm out buying stock or picking up a piece of land—things like that. I'd sure feel easier having you along with me then. . . . Seeing the way you handled yourself with Rutter and Pete and Rufe Mysak's what gave me the idea. You be interested in that kind of a job?"

Starbuck shifted in his chair. "Done it before, but I'm not exactly interested in a job—leastwise not until I've talked to Henry Smith. After that I'll know where I stand."

"What's Henry got to do with it?"

"Starbuck's a-lookin' for his brother," Gage explained. "Ain't seen him in ten year or better. Thinks maybe Henry's him."

Underwood stroked his closely shaved chin. "And if he is?"

Shawn said, "Means we've both got a long ride back to Ohio ahead of us."

"If not?"

"I start looking again."

The rancher smiled. "Then I don't see how putting you to work for me would interfere much with your plans. You could stay on for two, three months while things are busy for me and until I could find another man to take

56

your place. Then you could move on if you like. . . . Man living the way you are probably has to stop every now and then to build up his cash, anyway."

Shawn said, "You're right." He was more or less at that point now—but with Holly close by—running into her. . . .

"Pay'd be a hundred a month and found."

Starbuck swallowed. That was good money. Even if he worked only two or three months he'd have enough cash in his pockets to carry him on through winter. It was an offer he couldn't afford to turn down; where Holly was concerned he'd just have to keep looking the other way, keep his mind on his job.

"It's a deal. You've hired yourself a messenger boy, or whatever you want to call me. Want it understood, however, that if Henry Smith turns out to be my brother, it's all off."

"Fair enough," Underwood said, slapping the top of his desk. "You can bunk down—"

"He's staying in my cabin," Gage broke in. "After that go around he had with your friends, I figured he'd best not be in the same room with them."

"Good," the rancher said, rising to show that the interview was at an end. "Don't have anything particular for you to do at present, but hang around close, keep yourself available."

Shawn extended his hand, shook that of the rancher. His thoughts flipped back to the incident near the Indian ruins.

"There anything I should know—maybe about somebody I ought to watch out for or keep an eye on?"

Sam Underwood wagged his head. "Not a soul. Guess you might say I'm everybody's friend. I make a habit of keeping it that way."

◎ 10 ◎

Starbuck and Tom Gage were standing in front of the wagonshed late the next morning when Guy Rutter, flanked by Brock and a dozing Rufe Mysak, rode in. Immediately, the old foreman, eyes burning, stepped out to meet them.

"Where the hell you been?" he demanded.

Mysak came awake with a start. Rutter, mouth set to a crooked line, shrugged. "I reckon we're a mite late."

"You're damned right you are. You're supposed to be working, same as the rest of the hands on this ranch."

Brock rested his arms on the saddlehorn. "Maybe Mr. Underwood forgot to tell you we was taking us a little ride into town."

"He told me, but you was due to go to work this morning—early, just the same. How the hell you think I can run this place if the crew comes and goes when it damn well pleases?"

"Would be a problem," Brock admitted mildly. "You aim to give us a whipping?"

"Never mind, Pete," Rutter broke in, dismounting. He shifted his eyes to Shawn. "You're not much good at taking advice."

"Depends on the advice," Starbuck replied. "I—"

Gage, red-faced, pushed forward. "We ain't talking about him! We're talking about you and that pair of—"

"I said we was sorry, old man—"

"Sorry—hell! I'm telling Sam Underwood that he can—"

"Be telling him a few things myself."

"Then you can tell him I said you was fired—the lot of you! I won't have you around giving the rest of the crew ideas, making them think they ought to be acting like you."

Rutter's gaze settled on the foreman. Behind him Brock and Mysak had dismounted and were watching quietly.

"Now, we're trying to get along with you, Gage," the

58

redhead said, "but you're making it mighty hard. We aim to do our work, but we just had to pay us a little visit to town, see the elephant and such."

"You ain't ever going to get along with me till you start in doing your work, like you're supposed to."

Rutter nodded. "We're going to do that, but I was just thinking . . . you hadn't ought to go jumping all over us like you're doing. It ain't being nice to Sam's friends; and I just might mention to him that he ought to fire you, 'stead of you firing us."

"He won't have to fire me," Gage said in an anger-choked voice. "Anytime it's you calling the shots on this ranch, I quit. Now, *you* tell that to Sam when you see him!"

"Just what I'll do," the redhead said calmly, and then swung to Starbuck. "You had your warning, so now it'll be the hard way."

Turning on his heel, he walked off, followed by Brock and the glowering Mysak. At the front corral they left their horses, and moved on toward the main house. Gage watched them in fuming silence for a bit, then spun to Shawn.

"What's he talking about—you getting your warning, and doing things the hard way?"

"We had a few words. Gave me notice to ride on."

Tom Gage's fury soared again. "Why, that flapping-jawed jackass—who the hell he think he is spouting off with that kind of talk? I'll set him—"

"Don't bother," Starbuck said. "Met his kind before, probably run up against plenty just like him by the time I'm ready to die— Means nothing to me."

The kitchen door opened and Holly stepped out into the yard. Rufe Mysak slowed, raked her with his eyes, whistled softly. He said something to Rutter who only shook his head and continued on his way. The girl, paying no attention to them, moved farther into the yard, seemingly unaware of Mysak's persistent stare.

"Good morning!" she said brightly, walking in front of Shawn. "I hear you're taking a job with us after all. . . . I'm glad."

She gave him a wide smile, hurried on in her light, quick step for the barn where Manuel was leading out Amy Underwood's horse. Swinging to the saddle, she looked back to Starbuck.

"Promised Mother I'd take Blanco for a run today. She doesn't ride him near enough. Be pleased to have you come along."

Shawn nodded, touched the brim of his hat politely. "Obliged, but I'm a working hand now. Have to hang around close."

Holly tossed her head, swept out of the yard in a hammering of hooves. Tom Gage, his temper cooled, clucked softly.

"Like I told you, that gal sure has took a shine to you. Why don't you go on with her? Sam ain't needing you."

"Neither does she—somebody who can only cause her hurt."

"Pshaw—that ain't no way to talk. You're young. Ought to be thinking about the future."

"I've got no future—not the kind you're talking about —until I find Ben. . . . Can't you figure up a chore or two for me to do?"

Tom Gage was staring past Shawn toward the house. "Maybe I ain't the one who'll be telling anybody what to do around here from now on," he murmured.

Starbuck turned. Sam Underwood, with Rutter, Brock and Mysak in tow, was advancing across the hard pack. The rancher's features were strained, contrasting sharply with the settled, satisfied expression of Guy Rutter.

"Tom," Underwood began with no preliminaries. "Rutter tells me you jumped all over him and the boys for just coming in."

"You're damn well right I did!" the old foreman shot back, anger soaring again. "First thing you know the whole crew'll be thinking they can come and go as they please."

"I told you they had my permission to go to Vegas—"

"Ain't claiming you didn't. But they was due back here in time to go to work this morning, same as everybody else."

"I didn't set any time for them to return. Told you that, too."

"The hell you did, Sam! You said—"

"Well, I sure meant to. I'm sorry, Tom. Guess it just slipped my mind. . . . Anyway, it's all right."

"How can it be?" Gage demanded, thoroughly aroused. "You telling me to treat them privileged like, let the rest of the crew think they're something special, and better'n them?"

"Not exactly. But for the time being I want to make an exception—"

"Exception, hell! I'll tell you what you can do, Sam— you can get yourself another ramrod. I ain't never run a

60

place favoring some over others, and I ain't about to star now."

Underwood's face was white, drawn. "Now, hold on. Don't go off half-cocked."

"I'm done gone," the older man shouted. "I quit. Give me my time and I'll pull out. Then you can turn the job over to one of your special friends; let him do as he pleases."

"Sam," Mysak said, pushing forward. "I'd be real pleased to take on the job."

Underwood flashed the man an angry look, and laid his hand on Gage's shoulder. Worried lines cut deep into his features.

"Don't do this to me. I need you here. Fact is, I couldn't run this ranch without you."

"Then leave me alone, dammit! Keep your nose out of what's my business."

"What I intend to do—just like I always have. Whole thing's been a mix-up. And you won't need to worry about these fellows none. They'll work direct for me. Won't have anything to do with the rest of the hands."

Gage began to simmer down. After a moment he said, "Good enough. You keep them out of my hair, look after them yourself."

Underwood's eyes reflected his relief. Standing behind him Guy Rutter was silent, his features betraying no emotion of any sort. That he had merely wanted to put the old foreman in his place was apparent to Shawn.

"Then we've got it settled," the rancher said. "It be all right if they stay in the bunkhouse?"

"Nothing to me long as they mind their manners and keep their lips buttoned up."

"They'll do that," Underwood said with a sidelong glance at the three men.

Guy Rutter shrugged disinterestedly. Mysak winked broadly at Pete Brock. The rancher swung to face Starbuck.

"Got an errand for you. Something's come up, important that I get a letter quick to my partner in the bank, Ira Cameron. You be able to ride in an hour or so?"

"Whenever you say," Shawn replied, pleased that at last he had something to do.

Underwood deliberately turned his back to the other men, drew Starbuck aside. "Letter's more important than you might think," he said in a hushed, confidential way. "Don't be afraid to use that gun of yours getting it there —if need be."

61

Shawn signified his understanding. Guy Rutter was watching narrowly, he noted, a dark frown on his ruddy face.

"Be no hurry for you to return," Underwood said, his voice lifting to normal level again. "Stay the night, head home in the morning. Thing I'm interested in is that letter being put in Cameron's hands today."

Starbuck again nodded. A night in the settlement would be a welcome treat. A drink or two in one of the saloons, a few hands of cards—a man missed those things when he was on the trail day after day.

"Get my horse saddled," he said, turning for the corral.

Underwood also swung about, started for the house. "Be an hour or so. I'll sing out when I'm ready."

Rutter, with Brock and Mysak crowded up close to him, stood for a time watching the rancher move off, and then with a hard glance at Starbuck, headed for the bunkhouse. At once Tom Gage crossed to where Shawn was pulling tight a cinch.

"I ain't sure," the old foreman said, his eyes on the three men, "just what's going on around here, but you keep your eyes peeled while you're making that ride."

Shawn paused. "Meaning what?"

"Meaning I wouldn't trust them three saddlewarmers half as far as I could throw a cow barn—especially after that warning Rutter gave you."

"Way I feel about them," Starbuck said. "I'll be watching—going and coming."

◎ 11 ◎

Sam Underwood stood at the rear window that over-looked the yard and watched Guy Rutter, accompanied by Brock and Pete Mysak, ride off.

A feeling of satisfaction flowed through him. They were taking the bait he'd so carefully dangled in front of them, were doing exactly as he had hoped. Starbuck had been gone much less than an hour and already they were setting out to follow.

He had been certain they would. Rutter had a devious, suspicious mind and the letter—actually no more than some mortgage papers he'd brought home to read over and sign—would represent a possible double cross and a threat to the success of the bank holdup they planned.

Rutter would think he was tipping off Ira Cameron, in-structing him to call in the sheriff, set up an ambush inside the building. He'd not rest now until he got the letter in his hands, examined it and made sure.

That wouldn't be easy to accomplish. Starbuck, whom he'd impressed with the importance of the envelope and the need for delivering it at any and all costs, was not the sort to fail a trust; he'd fight. Rutter, even aided by Brock and the thick-skulled Mysak would be no match for an ex-pert gunslinger like him.

Thus it would come down to a shootout. Rutter, Brock and Mysak were bound to get the worst of it. He'd not be surprised if at least two of them ended up dead—and that was exactly what Sam Underwood wanted; two of them, or even one out of the picture, and there'd be no bank robbery. One man could not possibly pull off the job. . . . Two, perhaps, but the risk would be great, and Rutter, should he be one of those still alive, wasn't likely to take the chance.

He need not fear reprisal by way of the "girl" and the "letter" the three had mentioned, if indeed such a girl and

63

such a letter recounting the affair at Medford's Crossing existed. According to Rutter she'd been directed to hand the confession over to the law if there proved to be a trap awaiting them when the robbery was attempted. An unfortunate encounter with a gunman on the trail during which Rutter and the others got themselves shot to hell before any robbery attempt could hardly apply to the instructions that had been given her.

And by then he'd have had time to do a little investigating himself, learn who the girl was, and if there was a letter, get it by paying her off. Women of the sort Rutter would associate with always had a price, particularly when the man she'd made a deal with and expected a bonus of cash from was dead or wounded and unable to pay.

He'd worked it out carefully, thought it through to the end. Rutter and his buckos would discover they'd underestimated him, that they'd picked the wrong man to squeeze down on, try to blackmail. Hell, he hadn't got where he was by being stupid.

He hadn't been too obvious, not with either Starbuck or Rutter. He'd shown just enough secrecy there in the yard to pique Rutter, arouse his suspicions—and just the right amount of seriousness where Starbuck was concerned to impress him with the importance of fighting for the letter, if need be.

He would have liked to bring Starbuck a bit deeper into his scheme, actually warn him about Rutter, but that might have spoiled the whole thing. It was better if it all came off unexpectedly; a sudden attack by the three men, the quick and violent reaction of Starbuck protecting a most valuable envelope entrusted to his care. That's what he counted on. . . . He did hope Starbuck came out of it all right, though. He liked the young man.

He reckoned he didn't have to worry about Shawn Starbuck, however. He could take care of himself. One look into those cool, gray eyes, or at the way he handled himself even when the odds were all wrong, gave one the idea that he'd been down the road plenty and there was damned little that could faze him. Starbuck would come out on top—maybe with a bullet hole or two—but he'd make it, and he'd get the job done.

Regardless, in Sam Underwood's mind the result justified the means. He could not, under any circumstances, permit anything to stand in the way of getting what he desired most—the governorship of the Territory. The power and prestige that came with it meant everything to him and his family, as well as to a considerable number of fellow ranchers, businessmen and certain important politicians.

Actually, when you viewed it objectively, he would be breaking faith, letting them down if he didn't take drastic steps to block off any and all threats to the fulfillment of his plans. They were depending upon him, basing their futures on what he could do for them once he attained the Governor's Palace. It would be criminal to allow a ghost out of the past to wreck their hopes.

Underwood grinned wryly. He could expect some violent repercussions from Starbuck when it was all over and done with. The tall stranger had guessed that all was not rosy between him and his army pals. His meaning had been clear when he asked if there was anyone in particular he should keep an eye open for—and he had meant Guy Rutter, Mysak and Brock. . . . He was glad he'd had the presence of mind to deny any and all enemies.

Well, he'd play it that way right through to the finish. He'd make Starbuck—assuming he survived the trap Rutter and the others were certain to lay for him once they'd swung by and gotten ahead—believe that he had no idea of their intentions; that, as far as he was concerned, they were old, trusted friends and had fooled him completely.

Starbuck would believe it—or possibly, he would not since he wasn't the kind to be fooled easily; but if he didn't swallow the explanation—what of it? There was absolutely nothing he could do about anything.

Motion at the far side of the yard drew Underwood's attention. Tom Gage, coming in from the range where he'd been looking things over, no doubt. It had been touch and go with Tom there for a bit. For a few moments he thought he'd lost him—and that would have posed a serious problem.

As long as Tom Gage was around to run Underwood, he had no worries as far as the ranch was concerned. In fact, and he had freely admitted such to everyone, he'd realized a long time ago that he couldn't have made it to the top of the heap without the help of the crusty old cowman.

He must keep Tom satisfied and happy, humor him along, no matter what it took. Only then could he feel secure and know, after he became governor, that the ranch was not going to pot for lack of management.

But he guessed things were all right with the old foreman now. He'd cooled off when it appeared he was to have his way, and that there'd be no more interference from anyone. . . . He'd not allow an explosive situation like that to arise again—that was for sure.

Underwood watched Gage ride up to the corrals, halt and sit quietly staring at the horses in the front enclosure. The old man was sharp. Damned little got by him. He was noticing now the absence of the horses Rutter, Brock and Mysak used. He wouldn't guess, though, that the three men had ridden out to follow Starbuck—and meet their doom. He'd have no reason to think of such; he'd simply assume they were off somewhere, and forget it.

Taking a deep, satisfied breath, Sam Underwood looked off across the yard to the low hills beyond and smiled contentedly while through his mind passed this thought: *Mr. Governor-to-be, you've done yourself proud, climbing out of that mess. By the time this day's done you can forget Guy Rutter and Pete Brock and Rufe Mysak and Medford's Crossing, and start figuring who you're going to favor with all those fat appointments you'll be passing out after you're sworn in. Got to hand them over to those who can do you the most good. . . . You scratch my back, I'll scratch yours. It's a good rule.*

"Samuel. . . ."

Amy Underwood's voice reached him from an adjoining room. She always used his full name although he preferred the diminutive. Her genteel Southern upbringing, he supposed. But it did sound a bit more dignified and formal. Maybe, after the inauguration, he'd sort of start using it.

"Samuel?" Amy said again.

"Right here."

"I told Holly to invite the Camerons over for dinner Sunday. She'll stay over and ride back with them."

A frown clouded Underwood's face as he pivoted on a heel slowly. "Holly—did she go to Vegas?"

"Yes. . . . Was there something you wanted?"

A great fear was blossoming within the rancher. In a long stride he crossed the room to the connecting doorway.

"When did she leave?" he asked in a breathless voice.

Amy, comfortable in her pink velour rocker, looked up from her tatting. "An hour or so ago. That new man you hired was riding in—some business of yours, Holly said, and—"

"Starbuck? Did she go with Starbuck?"

"Why, yes, that's the name she mentioned. She had some shopping to do, asked if it would be all right to go with him. I told her yes, of course."

Sam Underwood stood frozen, eyes bright with shock, lower jaw sagging. Amy, a look of concern covering her face, rose, moved anxiously to his side.

"Wasn't it all right? Both you and Tom seemed to think this Starbuck is a fine, young man."

"Holly—oh, my God!" Underwood muttered as visions of what awaited her on the trail rocked through his mind.

"Did I do something wrong? She's ridden to town before with the hired hands. I couldn't see why—"

"Never mind," he said, the realities and necessities of the moment grasping him harshly. "Something I've got to do. . . . Don't wait supper for me."

In the next instant he had snatched up his hat, was running through the doorway into the yard, yelling for Manuel to get his horse saddled.

◎ 12 ◎

Starbuck, no more than a half mile from the Underwood ranch, caught the sound of hoofbeats in his wake. Instantly he swung the chestnut off into a dense tamarisk windbreak. Hand resting lightly on the butt of his pistol, he waited.

Soon, Holly, dressed in her corduroy riding outfit but this time wearing a man's wide-brimmed hat instead of the usual brightly colored scarf, broke into view. Her face was intent as she looked down the road.

Shawn moved out of the thicket, the tautness slipping from his long frame. "Hunting for me?"

Reining in sharply, she whirled, startled. A smile of relief parted her lips.

"I was afraid I'd missed you."

Shawn frowned. "Missed me?"

"I thought maybe you were farther ahead than I expected, and I'd have trouble catching up. . . . I'm riding in to Vegas, too."

Starbuck's brow puckered with disapproval. He wanted no company on this journey—particularly hers.

"Your father know about this?"

"He does by now. I told Mother. . . . There's nothing wrong with it. I often ride to town with the men." She studied him soberly as they continued down the road. "Why? Don't you want me along?"

"Not that," he replied, shifting on the saddle. "Happens I'm running an errand for your father. Important one, I guess. Aimed to travel fast and hard."

"I know. It's a letter to Ira Cameron at the bank. I overheard father talking to you. . . . That's where I stay— with the Camerons."

Shawn gazed ahead, settled himself resignedly on the chestnut. He didn't like the idea but he guessed it was all right—and there seemed little he could do about it, anyway. Almost curtly he bobbed his head in agreement.

"Let's go," he said and spurred the gelding to a fast lope.

She moved up beside him quickly, riding her sorrel with a flawless, natural grace. Abreast, the two horses, one only a slightly darker red than the other in the hot, afternoon sun, stretched out in a matching pace.

Some time later they were out of the trees and brush, were once again on open, grassy range. For a full hour they traveled across an almost level plain, and then the road began to rise toward the mountains in the distance. The grass thinned, became irregularly spaced clumps; the land began to break up with scatterings of rock here and there while rabbit brush, sage and groundsel became more plentiful.

Shawn glanced at Holly's sorrel and noted the lather flecking his coat. At once he began to slow, realizing he'd not given her mount thought, was gauging endurance and fitness by the standards of the powerful chestnut. Pulling into a trot, he brushed sweat from his forehead, shifted his attention to Holly. Her tanned, serene face was glistening from the heat but she had voiced no complaint, and made none now.

"Shade down there," he said, indicating a stand of small trees a quarter mile distant. "Be a good place to pull up, rest a bit."

The girl nodded, then pointed to a darker patch of green higher up on the slope above the road. "That's where we usually stop. There's a spring. We can get a cool drink, water the horses."

Shawn was not especially interested in any lengthy stop, and the chestnut was not in need of watering, but he had Holly to think of. Immediately he swung onto a narrow path that veered off the road, angled upward.

It was pleasant beneath the cottonwoods and chokecherrys. The grass was thick, a rich emerald, and the murmur of water bubbling from under a granite ledge, rushing over a bed of sand and pebbles for a dozen strides to disappear again into the dark earth, was soothing. Wild verbena lay like a purple mat on the nearby slopes and yellow crownbeard, standing in dense profusion, crowded the banks of the creek.

Under different circumstances Starbuck would have appreciated the mountain oasis, would have considered it a fine place to loaf away a summer's day, but with Sam Underwood's letter tucked inside his shirt, its sharp corners digging into his skin reminding him of its presence, dalliance must necessarily be limited.

"Best we move on," he said, getting to his feet. "Sooner I get this—"

Words died on his lips as the distant, hollow thud of running horses somewhere below came to him. Moving forward, he looked down slope. The spring lay in a fairly deep hollow and a long, rock-studded ridge shut off his view completely. He turned back to where Holly waited with the horses.

"Riders. Several, sounded like."

The girl swung to her saddle, not waiting for him to assist. "Lots of people use the road," she said. "Connects with the one that runs into Texas. Anyone going from there to Vegas or Santa Fe—any of the towns in the Rio Grande Valley, will use it."

"Don't think they were on the road. Seemed farther, below that, moving fast."

She smiled down at him, her eyes mischievous. "Taking a short cut. . . . Maybe they're anxious to get to town and see the saloon girls, too, like you."

"Not the reason I'm in a hurry," Starbuck said, stepping up onto the gelding.

Holly was probably right, he thought, and he should forget it, not become disturbed. But he found himself wondering about the riders as they worked their way back down the slope to the road. . . . It was that damned letter, he guessed. If Underwood hadn't gone so strong at impressing him of its importance and the absolute need for getting it delivered safely to Ira Cameron at the bank, he likely would not have given the passersby any consideration.

They reached the well-marked roadway, resumed the journey. Once again Starbuck set the pace at a good lope, but now his attention was on the country ahead. He should be able to glimpse the riders somewhere in the distance since the land rose and fell in a series of slopes and crests created by the higher ridges to the north.

He hoped Holly was right in her assumption—that what he had heard was only cowpunchers on their way to town for a spree, but the ingrained caution of the man would not permit him to accept such an explanation without some degree of reservation. Thus he continued to search the winding dust ribbon before him; he had to be sure.

He saw the three men a short time later. They were climbing a long grade somewhat below and parallel to the road. They were crowding their horses hard. The distance

70

was too great to make recognition possible, but suspicion rose instantly in Starbuck's mind, and when the riders dropped over onto the far side of the ridge, he swerved in close to Holly.

"There another way to Las Vegas besides this one? A trail, maybe?"

The girl shook her head. "Not that I ever heard of. They say the country in between is very rough—all canyons and buttes. Why?"

"Would as soon get off this road," he replied, and let it drop there, not wishing to alarm her unduly.

She glanced at him, a petulant frown on her face. "I thought it would be fun riding with you, Shawn. . . . You won't even talk, much less joke and cut up like the other hands."

"Wasn't my idea, your coming along."

Her face colored and her shoulders came back. "If that's how you feel I can go on alone," she said stiffly.

"Not saying that I feel that way. Just that this letter of your pa's is important—probably a lot more than you think."

She looked at him closely. "It's those riders you're worried about, isn't it?"

"Not especially worried—just being careful."

Holly shrugged. "I still think they're just cowboys going to town for a good time."

"And I'm hoping you're right," he said, but deep within him felt that she wasn't.

Not long after that they gained the summit of the long slope on which he'd caught first sight of the men. An equally lengthy distance below, the road entered a somewhat narrow passage hemmed in on both sides with rock and brush, and then again began to climb another slanting hillside.

Starbuck gave that some thought. The riders should be in view as they made their ascent. There was no one visible anywhere. Such could only mean they had stopped in the maze of tangled growth and boulders at the foot of the grade. Once more he swung in close to the sorrel.

"There water down there in the bottom?"

Holly shook her head. "That spring where we were, it's the only place between the ranch and Vegas."

Small warning flags began to wave inside Shawn Starbuck's brain. It sounded like an ambush. Underwood's warning had not been for nothing. Someone wanted the envelope he was carrying—bad.

He studied the country before him. The road angled to

71

the left, dropped off to a fairly steep slant as it snaked its way downward to the ragged arroyo at the junction of the two slopes. Alert, he continued on its course, following the rutted tracks to a point where they whipped back in a sharp bend and he knew that Holly and he would not be visible to anyone watching from below, and there cut abruptly away, taking to the rough, open land on their right.

"Where are you going?" Holly demanded, puzzled.

"Higher up. We'll keep in the hills," he explained. "Got a hunch those men are waiting for us at the foot of the slope. Not taking any chances. We'll circle around them."

Surprisingly, she did not protest, but simply swung off the road and followed him up a steep slide covered with loose shale, to a higher level. There they broke out onto a ridge, soon dropped off into a short, shallow valley that ran east and west, as did the road.

Coming to the far side, Starbuck rode to its lower rim, looked down. The arroyo was still a considerable distance in front of them. To bypass, as he planned, he would have to keep to the higher land for another mile at least.

With painstaking care he probed the slopes and little gullies before him. There was no deep swale now in which they could ride unseen, only a series of dangerous slides backed by towering bluffs. The horses would have hard going.

Moving out in front of Holly, he said, "Keep up close. If the sorrel starts spooking, we'll walk."

The girl's presence was a complication. Alone, the chances were he'd not take such trouble to avoid what possibly was no ambush at all but merely three men resting on their way to Las Vegas. But he couldn't afford to gamble on that; if it was a trap designed to stop him and take Sam Underwood's letter, and he rode into it, there'd be gunplay, and he couldn't risk Holly getting hurt.

Better to take all precautions, better to be sure. . . . He'd have a look, though, when they reached a point where he could see down into the arroyo clearly.

Starbuck knew it was an ambush well before that moment came. As he rode near the edge of a treacherously loose-surfaced bench, his eye caught the sudden bright flash of sunlight on metal in the brush. He pulled up short.

"What is it?" Holly asked instantly.

Shawn pointed at the undergrowth below. There was no reason now to hold anything back from her.

"Keep looking," he said.

72

It came again—the metallic glint just within the fringe of the brake.

"The riders we heard—they're holed up in there, waiting for us—for me. That was sunlight shining on a gun barrel."

She showed no sign of fear, but asked, "Who are they? You have any idea?"

Starbuck had a vague hunch, but no more than that. Therefore, he said, "Three men—about all I can say."

"What can we do?"

His attention swung back to the land facing them. "Can't keep going straight across, that's for sure. Buttes up there block the way. Have to angle down slope, get back on the road."

"They'll hear us—see us, too."

Shawn nodded. "How they had it figured, I expect. Hills coming together there, like they do, makes a natural pass. Only way through is by the road." He raised his glance to meet hers. "Be a good idea for you to double back, keep clear of this."

Holly's chin set itself firmly. "I'd feel better with you—safer."

Shawn thought back to those earlier moments in the yard at Underwood's when Rufe Mysak had first seen the girl and had swept her with his hungering appraisal. Keeping her close by where he could watch out for her would be better.

"Then listen close. Want you to stay on my right, in behind my horse until we reach that flat you see about a quarter mile below us. . . . We get there, you slap your spurs to that sorrel and head for the road. Once you're on it—don't stop until you reach town. Understand?"

She signified her agreement, but there was a frown on her face. "What are you going to do?"

His plan was to keep himself between her and the men in the brush, draw fire away from her, while at the same time he tried to pin them down with his own weapon.

But he said, "Sort of curious about them. Think I know who they are, but I aim to have myself a look, be sure."

The explanation satisfied her and they moved on, letting the horses pick their way over the uncertain, steep footing. Careful as they were, there was a continual dislodging of small rocks and a steady spilling of gravel. As they drew nearer to the flat strip of almost level ground Shawn had pointed out to Holly, he drew his pistol and rode with it in his hand. When they came to the little flat they would not be far from the arroyo.

73

The sudden, spiteful crack of a gun brought all thought, all speculation to an end. Shawn jerked the chestnut to one side, allowed Holly to crowd by onto the flat.

"Get out of here!" he yelled, and slapped the sorrel on the rump so that the horse leaped away and plunged off the low bank to the level racing for the road some fifty yards farther on. Starbuck, wheeling the gelding, fired blindly into the brush-filled arroyo. Again a pistol cracked. The bullet splatted dully into the bluff behind Shawn.

He was in a bad position—and an easy target. Throwing a hasty glance at Holly that assured him that she had gained the road and was quickly pulling out of danger, he cut back, pivoting so sharply the chestnut came up on his hind legs, and then jumped the horse off the ledge into a narrow wash several feet below.

Shots were coming in quick succession now, but he was in back of a mound of rock and no longer in the open as before. Two more guns began to blast. Apparently only one of the trio had spotted him and Holly at the start. The others, hiding elsewhere in the undergrowth—probably on the opposite side of the arroyo—had heard and come to add their support.

Bent low over his horse, he hurried along the floor of the gully, holding his return fire. The men in the brush continued to hammer the side of the hill where they had seen him last—thinking him still in the undergrowth. Abruptly he broke into the open. Instantly the pattern of shooting changed. A bullet sang off the metal horn of his saddle; another clipped the brim of his hat, while others spurted sand around the chestnut's hooves.

Cursing, he spurred the big horse ahead in a quick surge for the road, snapped two shots into the arroyo at the point where the firing seemed to come from. At once two horses shied out of the stunted trees and brushes onto a bare strip of ground at the base of the slope. His bullets had evidently hit close, frightening them. A man appeared, racing to grab the trailing reins of the animals before they could bolt.

Anger, but no surprise, ripped through Starbuck as he recognized Brock. Surely, Guy Rutter and Mysak would be the others who had lain in wait for him.

Emptying his pistol into the brush as he reached the hard surface of the road, he veered right. A shoulder of weed-covered earth closed him off from view of the arroyo. He took a deep breath as the shooting suddenly ended.

Pointing the chestnut up the long slope, he began to rod the spent cartridges from the cylinder of his forty-five, and thumb in fresh loads. . . . Sam Underwood was going to be surprised when he learned his army pals were far from friends.

◎ 13 ◎

Holly was waiting at the top of the hill.

"What the hell are you doing here?" he shouted, furious at her. Halting the chestnut, he twisted about, threw his glance down to the arroyo. Fortunately, Rutter and the others had not yet begun a pursuit.

"I told you to ride for town," he added, his manner softening.

The worried look on her face had faded. "I—I was afraid for you. I had to know—I had to wait."

"I'm fine," he said gruffly. "Let's move out. They'll be coming."

At once they cut into the road, here another long, flowing grade. The gelding was winded after his fast climb and Starbuck did not press him too hard. Their lead on the three would last for a time. If the men did close the gap, he wanted the gelding ready for another hard run.

"Who were they?"

Shawn had expected the question, and had been undecided at first as to how to answer it. For her own safety she should know.

"Guy Rutter and his sidekicks—Brock and Mysak."

Holly stared at him in astonishment. "You mean those friends of my father—the ones who came to see him?"

"Friends!" Starbuck echoed the word scornfully. "Can't call them that. They wanted this letter of your pa's so bad they didn't mind killing to get it."

The girl was silent for a full minute as the horses pounded steadily on. Then, "It's hard to believe."

"The hard thing to figure is how they can be friends of your pa's. Not the kind I'd expect him to have."

"It goes back to the war. They were in the same outfit. . . . I suppose that explains it. They were all right then, but they've changed."

76

"Somebody sure has," Starbuck muttered, more to himself than to Holly. "Are we far from town?"

"Only an hour or so. . . . What are you going to do about them?"

"Nothing—unless they keep pushing. I figure it's up to your pa. They're *his* problem."

"The sheriff should be told about it. You could have been killed."

He shrugged. "That's up to your pa, too. Was his letter they were after. Far as I'm concerned I'll look after myself."

There was still no sign of the others when Shawn and Holly reached the outskirts of Las Vegas and turned into the main street. As they rode down the wide, dusty channel between buildings, Holly pointed out the bank to him.

"You'll find Mr. Cameron there. . . . I'm going on to his house—spend the night with them." She hesitated and added impulsively, "Later, if you feel like it you could ride out to the Cameron place. It's at the far end of the town."

Shawn was unwilling to commit himself. The three men would show up, he was certain. They would arrive too late to stop delivery of the envelope, but that didn't mean he'd seen the last of them. They'd warned him earlier to move on; now they would have to silence him before he could report the attempted ambush to Sam Underwood. With him out of the way—and since Holly had not actually seen any of them—they could deny knowledge of the incident.

"I aim to check into the hotel, take things easy."

"Go to the Exchange," she said, pointing to a building a few doors on down from the bank. "It's the best."

"Want to give myself a good scrubbing, then see the sights."

Holly nodded, understanding probably more than he gave her credit for. "If you do take the notion, you'll be welcome at the Cameron's," she said, and rode on.

He swung into the hitchrack fronting the bank, halted and dismounted. Entering the low-ceilinged, shadow-filled building, he paused just inside the doorway and glanced around. To his left a lone teller dozed in his cage; to the right an elderly man sat at a desk behind a waist-high counter.

"You Ira Cameron?" he asked, moving up to the latter.

The man with the shock of snow-white hair got to his feet, a practiced smile on his lips. "I am. What can I do for you?"

77

Shawn dug into his shirt, produced the letter and passed it over. "Take this," he said, relief in his tone. "Rode in with it from Sam Underwood."

Cameron deftly slid an opener under the envelope's flap, glanced at its contents and tossed it onto his desk.

"Thank you," he said. "Something wrong with Sam?"

"No, just wanted to get that letter to you in a hurry. Sent me with it."

The banker shrugged. "Was no need for all the rush, Mr.——"

"Starbuck."

"Mr. Starbuck. Sam could have brought it in the next time he came to town. You a new hand at his place? Can't recall seeing you before."

Shawn puzzled, ignored the question, pointed instead to the letter. "You mean there's nothing important in that?"

"Only some mortgage forms, trust deeds and such. Ordinary bank business, that's all."

Anger whipped through Starbuck. *Nothing important!* Sam Underwood had led him to believe the envelope was vital—something he should be ready and willing to protect with his life, if necessary. His temper mounted higher. What the hell was going on? Why would the rancher lie about it? Moreover, why would Guy Rutter want the letter? What good would mortgage papers be to him and his friends? None of it made any sense.

Turning back to Cameron, he said, "If there's any answer or something you want taken back to Underwood, I'll be at the Exchange Hotel. Figure to spend the night."

"I'll remember that," Cameron said, moving back to his desk. "Obliged to you again."

Burning, Starbuck returned to the street. Stopping close to the wall of the building, he swept the dusty roadway with his glance. There was no sign of the three men. Then mounting, he rode to the stable at the rear of the hotel. Instructing the hostler as to the chestnut's care, he slung his saddlebags across his shoulder, doubled back to the front of the two-storied building and entered the lobby.

At the desk he registered, asked for and received a room facing the street, made his way to it. He stepped immediately to the window, swept back the frayed curtains. He had a fairly complete view of the road. Satisfied, he moved back, threw off his clothing and washed himself down from the china bowl and pitcher. He'd planned on a soak in a tin tub at the barber's but that was out now. He was too worked up over Underwood's deceit and Guy Rutter's attempt to ambush him. He had some accounting due from both; Underwood's he'd get when he returned to the ranch—Rutter when he showed up in town.

He took time to shave, and then drawing on the same clothes he was wearing when he rode in, went back to the street. For a time he lounged in the cool shade of the Exchange's gallery, idly watching the coming and going along the walks. . . . Las Vegas seemed a fairly busy town. There was hope, he'd heard someone say—Underwood, he thought—of a railroad soon.

Such would make the settlement the largest and most important city in the Territory, the rancher had said. No doubt it would be true—at least temporarily. What men like Underwood forgot and what he, personally, had noted in his wanderings, was that railroads never called a halt, had a habit of pushing their iron rails farther and farther, extending their reach to other towns, bringing to them greater size, importance and—usually—fleeting glory.

Weary of watching, waiting, Shawn moved off the hotel's porch and headed across the street for the ornate swinging doors of the Gold Dollar Saloon, easily the largest and apparently the most popular establishment of its kind in the settlement.

The last of the sun's rays were spraying a golden fan into the sky beyond the mountains to the west, tinting the windows of the shops and spreading a faint haze over the gradually cooling town. Here and there lamps had been lighted and a few storekeepers were locking their doors for the night.

A church bell was measuring off the hour—seven o'clock—in slow, mournful peals, and in the street adjacent to the saloon, a dusty mongrel was barking frantically at a buckskin-clad, bearded man entering on a starved-looking mule.

It was good to be in a town again, hear the sounds of people, smell the odors that reminded him of home, feel the presence of others bustling about at the business of everyday living. It had been some time since he'd found himself in anything larger than a ranch.

He'd make the best of it—Rutter and Underwood be damned. A few drinks to cut the dust and ease the tension that yet gripped him; then a good meal at one of the restaurants. Afterwards he'd go back to the Gold Dollar and while away the evening hours. . . . He wasn't forgetting about playing a few hands of cards, either; with the kind of money Underwood was paying him, he could afford to splurge a little.

He tried to put aside the thought of confronting Rutter

79

and the others. They hadn't put in an appearance so it would seem they were not anxious to meet him. Good enough, he'd find and settle with them later. . . . Right now live a little.

There was no need to worry about Holly. She would be with the Camerons, in good hands—not that her welfare was any concern of his, but he did feel sort of responsible for her after what had happened. . . . He could figure the night was his. He could relax, enjoy himself. Tomorrow would be soon enough to dig into the puzzle of why Underwood would send him on a useless errand that had almost gotten him killed, and why Guy Rutter had wanted so badly a letter of no value.

He reached the front of the Gold Dollar, halted, threw his glance back along the street for a final look. A half-dozen soldiers from Fort Union were coming into view at the north end of town. . . . A small boy with an apron that reached down to his shoe tops was sweeping the porch at Hayman's General Store. . . . A dozen or so persons sauntered along the sidewalks in the soft velvet twilight, soaking in the pleasant breeze drifting in from the high peaks of the Sangre de Cristos.

Satisfied and at ease, Shawn came back around, took a step toward the batwings. He halted abruptly as a man pushed hurriedly through, met him face to face.

Pete Brock. . . .

◎ 14 ◎

Starbuck's resolution to put his problems behind him vanished in a flare of anger. His hand dropped to the low-slung pistol on his hip.

"Don't move," he said harshly.

Brock's swollen, discolored features stiffened and a wild, apprehensive light came into his eyes. "Now hold on—wait a minute. . . . I—"

"Where're Rutter and Mysak?"

"Vida's room—inside—"

"Take me there—easy and quietlike."

Brock hesitated, cast a look to the right and then to his left in desperate hope of assistance. No one was watching. Starbuck's fingers tightened about the butt of his pistol and his free hand clenched into a fist.

"Now," he said softly.

Brock swallowed noisily, bobbed his head, and, turning, moved back into the saloon with Shawn crowding him. The smoke-hazed room was well filled with patrons, rocking with noise. In a far corner, barely audible above the lift and fall of the racket, a piano was being played.

Careful, alert, Starbuck followed Brock through the crowd. Several men turned, gave them brief attention during their passage, and then resumed whatever they were doing. Brock reached the foot of a stairway and slowed.

"This better not be a trick," Starbuck warned in a tight voice. "Not if you want to live."

"It ain't no trick!" Pete protested. "You said take you to Rutter. That's what I'm doing."

They mounted the steps to the second floor and entered a hall. Brock led the way down its shadowy length to a door at the extreme end, halted.

"In here. . . ."

Shawn nodded coldly. Drawing his pistol, he said: "Open it—step inside."

Brock hesitated uncertainly. Starbuck's balled fist came up. Instantly the outlaw reached for the knob. He gave it a twist, flung back the thin panel.

"Look out!" he shouted, and tried to duck to one side.

Starbuck's right slammed into the center of his shoulders, sent him plunging forward. Pete Mysak, almost directly in line with the door, sprang to his feet. Brock, off balance and under the force of Shawn's blow, crashed into the larger man. Both went sprawling to the floor.

In that same fragment of time Starbuck veered left and swung his gun like a club at Guy Rutter who had been sitting around a small table with the gaudily dressed Vida and Mysak. The blow caught Rutter on the side of the head as he clawed for his revolver, knocked him staggering into the wall as the woman yelled and leaped back.

Flushed with anger, breathing hard, Shawn kicked the door closed with a heel. Arms folded across his heaving chest, weapon hanging loosely in his hand, he surveyed the disorder.

The woman, a thick-waisted blonde with heavily rouged cheeks and vacant, colorless eyes, was drawn up against the back wall watching him with a fearful fascination.

Rutter, holding a hand to one side of his head, sagged against the adjacent partition, a burning hatred glowing in his stare. In the narrow space between the bed and the opposing wall, Brock and Mysak were untangling themselves, struggling to their feet.

"What the hell's this all about?" Guy Rutter demanded.

"Don't give me that!" Starbuck snarled. "Little matter of an ambush—one that didn't work. . . . I figure we ought to finish it—now."

A slyness filled the redhead's eyes. Keeping his hands well away from the pistol at his side, he drew himself erect, moved back to the chair he had so hastily vacated, and casually sat down.

"You ain't getting me to go for my gun," he said calmly. "Neither'll Pete or Rufe. You shoot, you'll be killing us in cold blood—and they hang a man in this town for that."

"Maybe. Odds are three to one, and you're all wearing guns. That might change a jury's thinking a bit." Shawn paused, swung his weapon slowly back and forth so as to cover all the men generally. "You want to stay alive, lift your pistols slowly with your left hand and drop them on the bed. . . . All of you."

Mysak swore vividly into the hot silence, did as ordered, and turned angrily to Brock.

82

"What the hell'd you bring him here for?" he shouted.

Brock rid himself of his weapon. "You think I done it a purpose?" he shot back. "Nailed me going out the front of the saloon—"

"You damned fool," Rutter snapped in a low, controlled voice. "I told you to keep out of sight."

"I was," Brock insisted. "Only going over to that store for a sack of Bull—"

"Sit down," Starbuck cut in. "On the floor—lean up against the wall," he added to Brock and Rufe Mysak.

Grumbling, the two men settled themselves on the scarred boards. Rutter slumped in his chair, one arm draped across the table. The woman—Vida—did not move. Shawn looked at her.

"You, too."

He righted the chair Mysak had occupied, shoved it up to the table with a foot. Vida pulled away from the wall, took her place next to Rutter.

Starbuck swept them all with his smoldering glance. "Now we get back to that ambush. . . . What was it all about?"

Mysak and Brock only stared. Rutter's lips drew into a scornful smile. Temper flared through Starbuck. He came away from the door against which he leaned, pistol ready in his left hand, right knotted into a big knuckled fist cocked and ready to strike. Guy Rutter jerked back, threw up both arms in fear.

"We wanted that letter you was carrying for Sam Underwood!" he cried.

"That's a goddam lie!" Starbuck replied. "Wasn't anything in that envelope but some mortgage papers."

Rutter's brows lifted as a look of incredulity crossed his face. He cast a sidelong glance at Pete and Rufe.

"That so?"

Shawn nodded. "It is. What did you think was in it?"

Again the redhead looked at his friends. "Well, uh—money. . . . A lot of money."

Starbuck swore in disgust. "A holdup," he muttered. "Robbing a man who figured you were his friends."

Mysak laughed, slapped his knee. "I guess we just ain't no-account!"

"Lower than that. . . . You could have killed Underwood's daughter, or got her hurt."

Rutter's manner was now indifferent. "Been too bad. Truth is, we weren't expecting her to be with you."

"But she was—and that didn't hold you back any. Figure I owe you for that, as well as for myself."

83

Rutter shrugged. "Up to you, but you ain't getting us into no fight. . . . What I'm thinking is you'd be smart to forget the whole thing. Tell Underwood, if you're of a mind, let him do what he likes—but you forget it. Nobody got hurt and you done the job you was hired to do. Ought to be satisfied."

"Not so sure that's all there is to it," Shawn said, thinking of Underwood. "What gave you the idea there was money in the envelope?"

"Sam did. Him telling you how important it was that it get delivered to the bank—and him sending it by you, his fancy gunslinger. Only natural we figure it was cash money. . . . You say there was nothing in it but papers, mortgages and stuff like that?"

"That's all."

Guy Rutter smiled. "Well, I'll be goddamned," he murmured. "Old Sam sure fooled us."

Fooled me, too, Starbuck thought bitterly, *almost into getting myself shot up.* . . . The rancher had better have some good reasons for what he had done.

"Reckon you can see now it was all a big mistake," Rutter said in an amiable tone. "Real sorry it happened. If you're willing, we'll just forget the whole thing."

"Seems I remember you ordering me to move on—"

"Forget that, too. Was a bit riled when I said it. I'm for letting that be bygones, too, if it's all right with you."

"Not a chance!" Starbuck rapped. "I'm getting some satisfaction, one way or another. You're all too gutless to stand up to me, so the next best thing is the law."

"The law—" Brock echoed, straightening.

"Sheriff's right here in Las Vegas. I'm filing charges against you for attempted holdup. Maybe I can even stretch it to attempted murder."

Rutter only smiled. "Best you talk that over with Sam Underwood first. How'd it look for him? A big man, head of the bank, getting all set to be the next governor—all cozy with somebody like us. Folks might start wondering just what kind of company he keeps was they to hear how his friends tried to rob him."

Pete Brock settled back. Mysak bobbed his bullet-shaped head. "That's a fact. Sure wouldn't help him none."

Shawn had a sudden impulse to give way to temper, start in on the three men, work them over good. But he knew it would accomplish nothing other than to salve the angry frustration that rankled him.

"Now, you talk to Sam about it," Rutter said in a self-assured manner. "Tell him what you're figuring to do. If he's agreeable to your going to the sheriff, you go ahead. We'll be right here. . . . We ain't planning on going no-where."

Starbuck, choking back the rage that was boiling through him, circled Rutter and the woman, gathered up the weapons lying on the bed. Holding them in a pocket shaped by his right arm, he backed to the door, opened it and stepped into the hall. Dropping the pistols to the floor, he booted them into a far corner.

"Don't step out here until you're damned sure I've gone," he said in a taut voice. "All I need is a little nudge to start shooting. . . . Already got plenty of reason."

Reaching for the knob, he drew the panel closed and wheeled back into the corridor.

◎ 15 ◎

Fuming, upset by his inability to satisfy the sense of outrage that claimed him; puzzled more than ever now by Sam Underwood's actions, Starbuck moved down the stairs, shouldered his way through the resounding clamor in the saloon and stepped out into the clean, cool night.

Nothing jibed. There was no sense of guilt in the three men for what they had attempted to do—and being the sort they were, he could understand that; it was the absolute lack of alarm, of fear they exhibited when he threatened to bring the law into the matter.

It was as if they were under some mysterious, powerful protection that would not permit the law or anyone else to punish them regardless of their crimes. They were willing to leave everything up to Sam Underwood even though they blandly admitted they had intended to rob him of money they thought he was sending to the bank.

Something was haywire somewhere—something that tied in directly with the rancher. He was the key, and the sooner he was confronted, forced to speak up and explain, the quicker the answers would be out.

Moving off the porch of the Gold Dollar, Starbuck grimly turned toward the Exchange. He'd not stay the night; he'd get the chestnut and head back to the ranch immediately. The way he felt he'd not get any sleep anyway.

His long stride slowed. A rider had turned into the south end of the street, horse limping badly. In the almost complete darkness the man looked familiar. Shawn's head came up abruptly. It was Underwood.

Rigid, he stepped off the board sidewalk into the dust, stalked toward the rancher in a purposeful line. A dozen paces short, Underwood recognized him, pulled up. The rancher's face was pale, strained, and his movements as he dropped from the saddle were anxious.

"My daughter—Holly—she all right?" he asked, hurrying forward.

Starbuck stared at the man coldly. "She is, no thanks to you. What's going on, mister? Speak up—I want to know —quick!"

Underwood's shoulders slumped in relief. He turned, led the horse to a close-by hitchrack, wrapped the reins around the bar and came slowly about.

Resting his weight on the crosspiece, he said: "Rutter and the others—they try to stop you?"

Shawn, holding tight to anger, nodded curtly. "You know damn well they did. Just happened I spotted them first, managed to slip by. You set up that ambush for me, didn't you?"

Underwood drew his handkerchief, mopped at his sweating features. "Guess you could say I did—in a way."

"Just what the hell does that mean?"

Two men passing along the walk on the opposite side of the street slowed, glanced curiously across, and then continued on their way.

"Didn't actually set it up—that is, I didn't tell Rutter and them to do it."

"You're beating around the bush, Mr. Underwood! I want the truth—all of it!"

The rancher again swabbed his face and neck. "Idea was to make Rutter think it was—well, valuable. The letter, I mean—the one I gave you to deliver."

"Then you figured he'd take out after me, set up an ambush and gun me down for it. . . . Why, in the name of—"

"Not you—them!" Underwood said in a sudden gust of words. "I thought you'd get them, being better with a gun —faster and with a lot of experience. None of them could even match you—alone or together. I knew that. It's what I was banking on."

Starbuck was studying the rancher in astonishment. "You mean I was supposed to kill them protecting that envelope?"

Sam Underwood bobbed his head weakly. "Seemed a good idea when I first thought it up. Was sure you could take care of yourself, come out on top."

"I'd probably be laying out there now, full of holes, if Holly hadn't suggested we turn off at the spring for a drink of water."

"Didn't know she was with you," Underwood said heavily. "Not until my wife mentioned it an hour or so after you pulled out. Grabbed my horse and followed fast as I could. Damned animal pulled up lame about ten miles out,

87

or I'd been here sooner. . . . Never been so worried in my life as I was when I learned Holly was with you."

"And I was riding into a trap," Shawn finished drily. "I'll tell you this, you came close to getting us both shot."

Underwood looked up quickly. "She know who they were?"

"She does. Was for me going straight to the sheriff about it. Told her they were your friends, that I'd leave it up to you. Getting a mite sorry I decided that way. They seem to think it's all a big joke."

"You've seen Rutter since?"

Starbuck jerked his thumb at the Gold Dollar. "In there, all of them. With a woman they call Vida. Tried to force them into a fight, settle a few scores, but they flat backed down."

"They say—anything special?"

"Laughed at me when I said I was going to the law since I couldn't even up things personally. Said I ought to tell you the whole thing because it was your property they were pulling the holdup for and your daughter who almost got hurt. Thought you ought to be the one to handle it with the sheriff. . . . Plenty sure of themselves."

Underwood stirred wearily. "Guess they are."

Starbuck crossed his arms, leaned forward slightly. Anger was still tightening his voice. "Got a hunch that's the answer to what this is all about. What makes them so damned sure? I want to know because whatever it is just about got me killed—and far as I'm concerned, I'm not done with them yet."

Underwood scrubbed nervously at his chin. "You could be, if you're willing to listen. . . . I'll pay you off. You can ride out, be on your way with a full month's wages. Job I hired you for is finished anyway, and—"

Shawn was shaking his head before the rancher had finished. "I don't like somebody throwing lead at me—and I don't like getting set up like a clay pigeon in a shooting gallery. . . . I'll pull out when I know what's behind all this, and after I've done some settling."

Sam Underwood lifted his hands, nodded woodenly. "Figured as much—you don't need to go on. And I reckon you've got a right. . . . First off, however, I'd like to see Holly, be sure she's—"

"Holly's fine," Starbuck cut in crisply. "Staying with the Camerons like she always does. Been there ever since we hit town."

The rancher's eyes traveled up and down the street, his expression desperate. Night had settled over Las Vegas and the saloons were all going full tilt with the Gold Dollar by far emitting the most racket.

"My horse—lame. Ought to see to him—"

Underwood was seeking escape, a way out, some excuse for delaying his explanation. Shawn eyed the man coldly.

"There's a stable behind the hotel. We can take him there. . . . Make up your mind to this, Underwood, you're not getting out of my reach until I hear what this is all about."

Abruptly the rancher seemed to wilt, shrink as if a tremendous weight had settled upon him. "All right," he said tonelessly, pulling the horse's reins free. "Let's get this animal to the stable, then go where we won't be bothered. . . . What I've got to say has never been told to anybody —not even to my wife."

◎ 16 ◎

"They're going to rob the bank—my bank," Sam Underwood said when, a short time later, they were in Starbuck's room at the Exchange. "Forcing me to help them."

Shawn, slumped in the solitary, battered chair his quarters afforded, watched the rancher pace nervously back and forth in front of the window. Out in the street there had been no lessening in the racket emanating from the saloons.

"Hell of it is, I can't do a damned thing about it. Tried tricking them, using you—but that backfired. Now I'm caught."

Starbuck leaned back, fingers interlaced across his belly. "Force you—how?"

Underwood's pacing ceased. His head tipped forward as his eyes studied the ragged carpeting on the floor. He seemed to be considering the question, making up his mind whether to answer or ignore it.

Shawn said, "If it ties in with your trying to get me shot up—I want an answer." There was no compromise in his voice, only a hard, unrelenting insistence.

The rancher raised his eyes, studied the tall rider for several moments, and then shrugged. "Guess I've got no choice," he said resignedly. "Have to tell you the whole thing. Goes way back."

"To the war."

"To the war," Underwood said. "We—Rutter, Mysak, Brock and another fellow named Gault—Billy Gault—he's dead now—we were all in the same outfit. Rutter was the leader of our bunch—the five of us. Used to prowl around together when we weren't on duty. Things had quieted down a good bit in the part of the country where we were stationed, and we had a lot of time on our hands.

"Well, one day Rutter heard about a paymaster's wagon passing through the area on its way to another camp. He

90

came up with the idea of robbing it. I was against it myself, but the war was coming to an end and we'd all be turned loose soon—dead broke, he kept telling us, and it was only right we grab what we could. Was the war's fault we'd be in the shape we'd be in—and on top of that none of us would have a job."

Underwood turned, stared through the window at a group of riders passing slowly by, heading out of town. One had consumed far more than his capacity of liquor and the man next him was struggling to hold him to his saddle.

"Was a damned fool to listen to Guy, but you know how things are at a time like that—when you're part of a bunch, I mean. You sort of have to go along with the rest. . . . Well, we ambushed the paymaster's wagon. A couple of soldiers got killed—actually three—and we ended up with the money. Was around six thousand dollars apiece.

"We stashed the money near camp and took turns keeping an eye on it. A few months later we were all discharged. We got together, dug up the sack and split the cash, then went our own way."

"Didn't the army look into the robbery, make an investigation or anything?" Starbuck asked, frowning.

"Oh, sure. There was a hell of a ruckus over it. For a while we had more brass in camp than we had regular soldiers. Then somebody came up with the information that Rebs had been seen in the neighborhood about the time it all happened, so everybody just assumed they were the ones who did it, and it all blew over. . . . Never did know for sure but I always had a hunch it was Rutter who started that rumor about the Rebs.

"I headed out west, ended up in this country. I used my six thousand to buy up a ranch, get myself started in the cattle business. Always told myself I'd send that six thousand back to the government someday, with a letter explaining where it came from—"

"Were you signing your name to it?"

Underwood shook his head. "No, couldn't very well do that, of course. There was those men killed trying to protect the wagon—I wasn't one of them that pulled a trigger, but I was in on it just the same. . . . Thing's bothered me a lot in the last few years. Should have sent the money back—things went good for me and I could spare it easy, but somehow I just never did. Now, I sure wish—"

"Wouldn't have meant much without your name to it," Starbuck said.

"Would've had it off my conscience—"

"The money, maybe, but not the killing of those soldiers —or the thing itself. . . . You ever see Rutter and the others again after that?"

"Not until they rode into my place a couple of days ago. Thought they were behind me for good, but seems they heard my name mentioned somewhere. Natural, me being boosted for governor and all that, and then owning a big ranch and part owner of a bank, and so on.

"They'd run through their share of the money a long time ago and had evidently been getting more by pulling off small-time holdups and robberies. When they got a line on me, Rutter come up with one of his smart ideas. They'd blackmail me into helping them rob my own bank." He reached into his pocket, produced a thick gold watch and looked at it. He peered out the window, wiping the sweat from his brow with his handkerchief.

"Anyway, Guy's plenty sly. When he found out where I stood in the Territory, he knew he had me by the short hair. He wrote a letter confessing to the robbery of that paymaster wagon, telling all about it—naming names—the whole works. Even dug up some of the old newspaper clippings that told when and where it took place, put it all in an envelope and addressed it to the U.S. Marshal.

"Then they came to the ranch, same day you showed up, told me if I didn't string along with their plan or tried to double-cross them, the letter would be handed over to the law. . . . That would fix me for good."

"That when you got this idea of sending me up against them, using that letter to Cameron as bait?"

The rancher looked anxiously again through the window and nodded. "Was a fool thing to do, suck you into it, but I reckon I wasn't thinking straight. All I could see was what it would do to me politically—and how it would ruin my family. Felt I had to stop Rutter somehow.

"I couldn't go to the law, of course. Guy had given the confession and clippings to his woman to hold—expect she's the one you saw—told her to hand it over to the sheriff if anything goes wrong during the robbery and they don't come out of it alive."

"Could be a bluff."

"No chance. There's a letter. I know Guy Rutter—his mind works that way. If he got himself killed robbing the bank, he'd get even by dragging me down. He's that kind of a man. That's the reason why I've had to go along with him and the others. Scared not to. Like I said, they've got me right where they want me. All I can do is squirm. They figure to pull off this bank robbery, lay low on my place for a time. I'm their protection. It happens somebody spots any of them pulling the job, I've got to say they're hired hands of mine, that I know for a fact they haven't been off the ranch."

Underwood moved to the bed and sank heavily upon its edge. Hands clasped, shoulders slumped, he stared at the floor in complete dejection. Shawn considered the rancher thoughtfully. He could hold no good feeling for this man, for the things he had done, yet a thread of pity stirred through him.

"When's the robbery coming off?" he asked.

"Tonight," Underwood said in a flat, helpless voice. "It's almost time now. Lot of money in the safe this part of the month. Probably near a hundred thousand dollars."

Starbuck swore under his breath. Why in heaven's name was he getting himself involved in situations like this? All he wanted to do was find Ben, clear up some problems concerning his own life. . . .

One thing was clear. He knew now why Guy Rutter and his two friends were so cocksure, why they were unafraid of repercussions from the law. They had Sam Underwood in a position where he must either go along with their plans, or else bare his past to the world and thereby commit political as well as personal suicide.

But there was more to it than that. Robbing the Las Vegas bank meant disaster to others—businessmen, ranchers, homesteaders, ordinary persons who kept their hard-earned money in its vault. To stand by and permit that to happen was to countenance a crime that would have far-reaching effects—and Shawn knew he could not have that on his conscience.

Sam Underwood had a duty to perform, an accounting to face. It would be bad, especially for Holly and Mrs. Underwood, but there was no other way out; one thing every man had to do eventually was pay for bed and board—and Underwood's time had come.

"You got only one choice," Starbuck said. "To go to the sheriff, bring him in on the deal."

The rancher's head came up slowly. "I'd have to admit —tell—"

"Yes. But down deep you knew someday you'd have to answer for that holdup."

"Yes—I guess I did. Only, there's my family—all my big plans for the Territory—"

"Be tough, not denying that, but I can't see where there's anything else you can do. Robbery was a long time ago—during wartime. That might change the way the law will look at it some. . . . And you'll get credit for the good things you've done. Far as your family's concerned they'll stand by you. But you'd better forget about being governor, even if they turn you loose. Folks like to think their statesmen are without fault—and I reckon they're right."

"They won't turn me loose. You're forgetting about those men that got killed. They'd send me to prison for that—maybe hang me."

"Risk you'll have to take. Point is, you can't let Rutter and them go through with the robbery."

Underwood shifted nervously. "There must be some way of stopping them and still not ruin everything," he said in a desperate voice.

"Don't see how you're going to do anything without owning up to—"

"Wait!" the rancher exclaimed, leaping to his feet. "Just come to me—!"

Starbuck eyed the man coldly. "If you're figuring on me —don't."

"But I'll have to. Only way I can keep them from doing it!" Underwood reached into his pocket and pulled out his watch again. "Got about a half hour before they start."

Shawn was studying the rancher's flushed face. He was into Underwood's problems just about as deep as he was going to go, and the thought of how the man had used him, deliberately set him up, still irked. . . . But if there was going to be an attempt made to rob the bank within thirty minutes, he was obligated to do what he could to stop it—like it or not.

"What's this idea of yours?"

"We'll keep them from doing it," Underwood said in a sudden rush of words. "You and me. We can slip in the bank by the back door—"

Starbuck's hands came up angrily. "No! We get the sheriff—bring him in—"

"There isn't time! I don't think Abrams is even in town, and I don't want to fool with a deputy. No time to do any organizing, have an armed party waiting. The two of us will be enough, anyway. Just three of them, and we'll have surprise on our side."

Wary, Shawn said, "We catch them, then what? You're still going to have to tell the law the whole story, because Rutter sure as hell will."

The rancher nodded slowly. "Guess there's no way around that. Like you said, I'll just have to take my

94

chances, hope everything doesn't go down a rat hole. . . .
You willing to give me a hand?"

Starbuck got to his feet. "I'll help, long as you aim to square yourself. . . . Not much time left. We'd better be getting over there. Rutter'll probably be keeping an eye on the place in case you've changed your mind. There a back way to the bank?"

"He won't be watching—not Rutter," Underwood said, moving toward the door. "He's dead sure of me. Figures I'll do exactly what he told me to. . . . But we can use the side entrance to the hotel, go down the alley. Nobody'll see us."

Starbuck hitched at his gun belt. "Let's get over there."

◎ 17 ◎

Underwood led the way down the almost totally black alley to the rear of the bank. It was not difficult for Shawn to understand why the others had chosen that hour of the evening for the robbery. The noise along the street was of such volume that little else, including gunfire, would be heard.

The rancher produced a key and opened the door; they entered. The building smelled dry, and the heat trapped within its walls was stifling. Closing and locking the panel, Underwood moved forward into a small, cleared area in which were two desks and several chairs.

In the dim light filtering through the window that faced the street, Starbuck could see the teller's cage to his right; he saw that he was behind the counter where Ira Cameron had stood when he had delivered Underwood's letter.

"Where's the safe?" he asked in a low voice.

The rancher crossed to a door beyond Cameron's desk. It appeared to be the entrance to a closet but when he drew it open, the black, iron face of a vault was visible.

"They'll be using blasting powder on that," Starbuck commented.

"What they figure to do. Mysak's sort of an expert on it. Was his job in the war—blowing up bridges and houses —things like that. He'll manage it easy."

And being a man experienced with explosives it was likely no one would hear it, Shawn thought. The correct amount of powder affixed to the safe's knob, the door quickly closed and buttressed with a desk, and the noise would be so effectively muffled that no one would be aware of what was taking place.

Starbuck looked more closely at the furnishings, now becoming distinct as his eyes adjusted to the dimness. He pointed to a short counter jutting off at right angles to the teller's barred compartment.

"One of us can hide behind that. Other ought to be on the opposite side of the room. They'll gather in front of the safe. We can cover them from two sides."

"Good," Underwood said, and took up a position back of the counter.

Shawn moved to the far side of the area. There was nothing similar there to employ as cover, and dragging one of the desks around until it faced the safe closet, he crouched behind it. He could watch both front and rear entrances as well as the vault from that point.

Hunkered in the darkness, he tried to figure how the outlaws would gain entry and prepare himself accordingly. It wasn't likely they would attempt to break through the front. Although most of Las Vegas seemed to be indoors, either in the saloons or their homes, a few persons were strolling along the sidewalks, and the crash of breaking glass would certainly draw attention.

It was logical to assume Rutter and his friends would come in from the rear, prying the thick panel from its hinges, or possibly daring to use an axe. They'd run no great risk, working from the alley where they would certainly never be seen and very probably not heard.

The problem settled in his mind, Shawn drew his revolver, checked its loads. There should be no cause to use it unless the men proved to be fools, tried to fight. And they weren't likely to do that—not with two guns pinning them down from opposite sides, trapping them in what could be a murderous cross-fire.

Starbuck raised himself partly, looked toward Underwood. "When you see me stand up—do the same," he called softly. "Let them know quick they're covered by the two of us."

"I'll be ready," the rancher replied.

Keeping his weapon in hand, Shawn leaned back against the wall, taking the strain off his leg muscles which were beginning to ache from the squatting position he was forced to assume. Noise from the Gold Dollar, almost directly across the street, seeped into the darkened room in steady waves, filling it with muted shouts, laughter, the dull thump of a piano. . . .

Starbuck tensed. There was a sound at the rear door. He braced himself, planting his feet squarely that he might rise swiftly and on balance. A ripple of surprise rolled through him. A key had grated in the lock. The faint squeak of hinges sounded and then came a stir of fresh, cool air as the panel swung open.

A key!

There was only one answer for that. Underwood had given it to them—forced to, he'd claim. Disgust curled Starbuck's lips. The rancher might as well have gone all the way—opened the safe and had the money ready for them.

A faint scuffing of boots and the thud of heels reached him. Rutter, Brock and Mysak, the latter two carrying sacks of some sort, were suddenly in the center of the room. They tarried a moment there, then crossed to the door behind Cameron's desk. Rutter opened it wide, stepped back, made a sweeping motion with his arm.

"Get at it, Rufe."

The thick-bodied man dropped to a crouch before the dully gleaming iron panel with its nickeled trimming. He examined the knob and handle briefly.

"Going to be easy," he said.

"What I told you, wasn't it?" Rutter said in a quick, impatient way. "Now, we got everything straight? Soon's that safe's open, you and Pete grab all the money you can find, stuff it into the bag. I'll keep standing watch close to the window, keep an eye peeled in case somebody heard the powder going off."

"You still want to head straight for Underwood's instead of north to Denver?" Brock asked.

"Underwood's," Rutter said. "Be the smartest move. We head for Denver we could run into the law—this town's got a telegraph office. Best we do like we planned, make out we're working for Sam."

"Save your breath," Starbuck said, rising to his full height from behind the desk. "You're going nowhere. . . . Keep your hands up—high, so I can see them—"

Brock was the one to make the first wrong move. He yelled something, dodged to one side, his pistol shattering the heat-laden hush. Shawn drove a bullet at the outlaw's shifting shadow, triggered another at Mysak, leveling down at him.

"Open up!" he yelled to Underwood.

Mysak went down in a heap, and then the room was in a haze of boiling smoke. Shawn could locate neither Brock nor Rutter, but they had him placed. Two more shots blasted deafeningly in the room. Leaden slugs splintered the surface of the desk back of which he crouched.

Why the hell didn't Underwood give him some help? A cross fire would force the men to surrender immediately.

One thing certain—he couldn't stay were he was. He doubted they could see him anymore than he could locate them in the swirling murk, but they did have his position

98

spotted and eventually one of them would get lucky. Bent low, under the thick-layered cover of smoke, he lunged across the intervening space to the counter where Sam Underwood had taken a stand. The rancher, pistol in hand, saw him, jerked back.

"No!" he cried in a hoarse wisper. "You'll draw their fire. . . . Get away—"

"What the hell's the matter with you?" Starbuck demanded in a savage voice. "Shoot—dammit! We'd had them cold if you'd shown yourself."

"I—I can't," Underwood moaned, shaking his head. "Too much at stake—to lose. . . . Can't risk it. . . . All up to you. . . ."

A dark shape loomed up in the haze directly in front of the counter. A gun blossomed bright orange in the darkness and a hot iron seared across Shawn's left wrist. He fired instinctively. Pete Brock yelled in pain and staggered. Reflex action triggered the weapon clutched in his hand twice, sent dual bullets smashing into the window of the bank. The glass fell to the floor with a loud crash.

Starbuck, belly flat, crawled clear of the counter and the cringing Sam Underwood. Rutter was somewhere in the gloom. His hand struck something yielding. . . . Brock's lifeless body. Groping about, he found the pistol. Picking it up, he tossed it into a far corner.

Instantly a gun blazed from the shelter of the closet in which stood the safe. Shawn's answering shot followed so quickly it was like an echo.

"Don't shoot—I'm hit!" Rutter's voice was high pitched, laced with fear and pain.

"Throw your gun through the window," Starbuck ordered. "Then walk out where I can see you

There was a thud as Rutter's pistol struck the wall below the opening of jagged glass, dropped to the floor. A moment later the outlaw staggered into view, one hand clutched to his side.

"I'll take care of him." Underwood's husky voice was strong at Starbuck's elbow. "Get over to the saloon and find that woman. Got to have that letter."

Several dim shapes in the street were moving cautiously toward the front of the bank, evidently not sure yet that it was safe to draw near.

"What difference does that damned letter make now?" Starbuck snarled. The rancher's courage had returned with amazing swiftness. "You're telling the whole thing to the sheriff, anyway."

"Just it," Underwood said in an urgent tone. "Want to

do the telling myself. Don't want him finding out that way."

Shawn was silent for a moment. Then, "Probably would be better. . . . . If I see the sheriff out there, I'll send him in."

"Go out the back," Underwood said hastily as Starbuck moved toward the opening in the window. "Some fool might take you for a holdup man and shoot you."

Shawn nodded, wheeled about.

"Don't lose time," the rancher called after him. "Be like her to make a run for the sheriff's office minute she hears what happened."

Starbuck made no reply, simply turned when he stepped into the alley, and trotted for the street.

◎ **18** ◎

As Starbuck hurried along the narrow passageway that separated the bank from its adjacent neighbor, two quick gunshots echoed across the clamor of the night. He gave that brief wonder, turned into the street, and strode for the brightly lit front of the Gold Dollar.

Men were crowding past the batwings, collecting on the porch, yelling questions at those converging gingerly on the bank. Others were running up from different points along the roadway, and somewhere a voice was shouting, "Abrams! Anybody seen Abrams around?"

Shawn stepped up onto the gallery, bulled his way against the current and entered the saloon. Moving to one side, he swung his glance around the room in search of Vida. He located her at a corner table, seemingly undisturbed by the mounting excitement. A puncher, very drunk, was beside her.

Crossing the littered area in long strides, Starbuck halted before her. "Upstairs," he said gruffly, jerking his thumb toward the second floor.

Vida stared at him dully from her lifeless eyes. The puncher stirred, raised his head, attempted to focus his gaze on Shawn. Failing, he lapsed again into a state of semiconsciousness. The woman shrugged, glanced at her partner.

"Why not?" she muttered thickly. "Your money's good as his."

Rising, she led the way across the saloon dance floor, up the stairs to the corridor, and on to her room. Once inside, Starbuck closed the door, turned the key. Vida, a fixed smile on her slack lips, wheeled expectantly, faced him.

"Seen you before, cowboy," she began. "You ain't never been—"

Starbuck's hard words cut her off. "I want that letter Rutter gave you."

Life stirred in her eyes. A frown knotted her brow as the lines in her face cut deeper. Abruptly her mouth fell open. She drew back a step.

"You're the one that come busting in here, raising hell with—"

"Where's that letter?"

A coyness slipped into her. She was drunk but not so far gone as to have lost her slyness.

"Don't know what you're talking about. . . ."

Starbuck seized her arm, shook her roughly. A comb fell from her hair, loosening several thick strands that spilled down around her shoulders.

"The hell you don't! I'm giving you one minute to hand over that letter or I'm taking this room apart—you along with it."

Vida looked down. "I ain't got no letter," she muttered sullenly.

"Don't tell me that. Rutter said he gave it to you—told you to take it to the sheriff if he didn't make it back. He won't. He's shot up plenty bad. Brock and Mysak are dead. You want to stay out of trouble, you'll fork it over —quick."

Vida was staring at him woodenly. "Dead?"

"All but Rutter. He'll live to go to jail—maybe hang."

She pulled back further, sat down on the creaky bed, eyes fixed on the tattered, faded paper covering the wall.

"Told him it wouldn't work. . . . Told him," she mumbled.

Shawn grasped her shoulder, again shook her. "That letter—where is it?"

A hardness wiped away the slack in her face as she looked up. "How much it worth to you?"

"Not a cent. Means nothing to me. I'm here for somebody else."

There was a loud burst of cheers down in the saloon, more in the street. Horses pounded up, stopped.

"You're from that rich sonofabitch who's wanting to be the governor—that's who you're from. . . . Ought to be worth a-plenty to him, the way Guy talked."

"Maybe it is. Up to him to decide that—and you can do your horse trading with him later. Right now I want that envelope."

"And trust him to pay me later? No, sir, not me! They're the worst kind—them rich ones. Bastards are always out to skin you. You go get him—"

Shawn stepped in close, caught the woman's dress by its low neckline, drew it taut.

102

"Expect I know where you're hiding it. You want me to rip off this rag, get it myself?"

Vida glared at him angrily, shook her head. "All right," she said, pushing his hand away. "You can have the goddam thing."

Thrusting her fingers deep into the cleavage between her ample breasts, she produced a folded envelope, passed it to him. Shawn glanced at the writing on its front. It was addressed simply: U.S. Marshal or Sheriff. As Underwood had predicted, Guy Rutter had not been bluffing.

Tucking the letter inside his shirt, he turned for the door. Vida's coarse voice lashed out at him.

"You tell that bastard I'm looking for him to pay me for that—you hear?"

Starbuck jerked the door back, said, "I'll tell him," and halted. The drunk Vida had been entertaining at the table was just reaching for the knob. Off balance, he swayed forward, caught himself by clutching the door frame.

"Say—where—" he began protestingly.

"She's all yours, friend," Shawn said, and taking the man by the shoulders, spun him into the room.

He walked the length of the corridor, went down the stairs. There appeared to be more of a crowd inside the saloon now than before, most of which was clustered about a man who was speaking excitedly.

"Was three of them. . . ." Starbuck caught the words as he drew abreast the tightly packed group. "Was all set to blast the door off'n the safe. Bag of powder's laying right there."

"And Sam got them all?"

"Every cussed one of them. . . . Seems he just happened by, seen them moving around inside, so he slips in the back way and throws down on them. Well, they decided to fight it out—and they sure got themselves into a dandy. Sam nailed all of them."

Shawn had come to a full stop. . . . *Sam got all of them!* The rancher was taking credit for the whole affair, but more than that—it sounded as if Rutter also was dead. Suddenly the meaning of the two gunshots he'd heard became clear to Starbuck. Underwood had shot him. Either Rutter had attempted to escape—or had been cut down in cold blood.

Bitterness filled Shawn's mouth. If that was it, then Sam Underwood had done it for one reason only—to silence Rutter to prevent his telling of the past. He swore silently. He'd been played for a fool again—and by the same man! The rancher had never intended going to the sheriff, making a clean breast of the past; he'd only wanted to get the three out of the way, and had persuaded him to help on the strength of a promise.

He'd been a fool. He should have realized why Underwood was so insistent that he leave the bank after the shooting; he'd made it appear he was anxious to get his hands on the letter Rutter had written. Undoubtedly he was, but he was more interested in being left alone with the wounded outlaw.

And the letter. . . . Starbuck reached into his shirt, felt it with his fingers as he continued on toward the doorway. Should he turn it over to the law? He stood there on the saloon porch deliberating the idea as commotion and noise continued to claim the street.

Several carriages had arrived. Spotted among the shifting throng were several soldiers. Lamps had been lighted inside the bank and Shawn could see a considerable number of persons had gathered there.

Maybe it wasn't exactly the way he'd figured; maybe he was jumping to conclusions too fast—and he should give Underwood the benefit of the doubt. It was possible Rutter had tried to escape and the rancher had been forced to kill him—just as it was also possible the man in the saloon had gotten some of his facts garbled in that he had given Sam Underwood full and solitary credit for preventing the robbery.

He reckoned he'd better hear things firsthand before he started condemning Underwood, and made any rash decisions as to the letter.

Descending the gallery, he waded through the milling crowd and worked his way toward the bank. Onlookers were ten deep in front of the shattered window, and he veered aside, moved back to the passageway he had used earlier.

Turning into it, he gained the alley. It was deserted, and cutting left he made his way to the rear entrance to the bank. A figure stepped from the shadows just within the doorway, barred his progress; a small, thin man with a rifle and wearing a deputy's star.

"Where you think you're going?" he demanded, lifting his weapon.

"Inside," Starbuck answered, faintly angered.

"Like hell you are. Ain't nobody going—"

"I'm with Sam Underwood. Name's Starbuck."

The deputy half turned, yelled, "Mr. Underwood, man back here named Starbuck. Says he's with you."

A lull in the drone of conversation settled over the

room at the lawman's call. Shawn saw the rancher look back, make an indifferent gesture.

"It's all right, Harvey. He's one of my hired hands."

The deputy pulled back. Starbuck walked toward the rancher and the group clustered around him. Holly was there, along with a younger girl and an elderly woman. The Camerons, he supposed. The banker himself was near the doorway, holding the panel open for several men who were carrying out the bodies of the outlaws.

Shawn halted behind Underwood. The rancher had resumed where he had broken off when the deputy interrupted, was talking in a steady, flowing stream. Holly, her face glowing, glanced to Starbuck and smiled proudly.

"Took a lot of nerve, Sam," someone in the crowd said, "standing up to three killers the way you did."

"Man does what he has to—when he has to," the rancher replied. "Couldn't just back off—and there wasn't time to get help."

"Well, you sure saved our hides," another commented. "Hate to think of what a robbery like that would've done to this town."

"Busted us all—that's for sure."

"We all owe Sam a lot for what he's done. . . ."

Underwood laughed, raised his hands. "You got to remember, there's money of mine in that safe, too. They'd have got it along with everybody's else's—and I didn't want that to happen."

Everyone laughed heartily except Shawn Starbuck. Silent, he listened to the comments while a wary scorn built up within him. The man in the saloon had been relating correctly; alone, Sam Underwood had come upon the outlaws, and unaided, challenged them, and when they resisted, shot them down in a gun duel.

Sam Underwood. . . . The town hero. . . . He'd be a cinch to sit in the governor's chair now. The local newspaper would plaster the Territory with a vivid, elaborate account of the incident. Underwood's niche was assured—as well as the exalted position he apparently felt was worth any cost to achieve.

Again the need to be fair and honest put a tight rein on Starbuck's thoughts. He could be wrong in this, too; Underwood was taking all the credit for himself perhaps only to enhance his reputation and prepare for the moment when he would make known the facts of his past. That could be the explanation.

The rancher could be planning, after all, to hand the letter over to the sheriff or the marshal, and being a mas-

105

ter politician, was simply striving to improve his image and lay the groundwork for a sympathetic hearing of his crimes.

Maybe that was it, and he should give the man—fighting desperately to prevent the empire he'd built from crumbling to dust—the benefit of the doubt, at least for the time being. As far as any credit for the killing of the outlaws was concerned, Starbuck could care less. Let Sam Underwood claim it, glory in it, make the most of it if it suited his fancy. . . . All he was interested in was seeing that right was done.

Shawn became aware of a dwindling in the conversation, of the fact that the rancher, deigning now to notice him, had stepped back.

"You get the letter?" Underwood's question was low, the words coming from the corner of his mouth.

"I got it," Starbuck drawled.

The rancher edged closer. "Slip it into my side pocket. Don't want anybody seeing it. . . ."

"No, I reckon not," Shawn said. "Figured I'd better hang onto it until you're ready to talk to the law."

Sam Underwood stiffened. "Now—hold on here. I—"

"I'll be at the hotel," Starbuck said, and pushing by the rancher, past Holly, and the others in the room, he moved through the doorway into the street.

◎ 19 ◎

In less than an hour, probably the minimum time it required for him to slip away from his throng of admirers, Sam Underwood rapped on Starbuck's door.

Shawn, again slumped in the lone chair, but placed this time near the window so that he could face the entrance to the room, stirred restlessly. He thoroughly disliked the role he found himself in—that of custodian of a man's future—but it had been thrust upon him and he could not in conscience turn away.

"It's open," he called.

The scarred panel flung back and the rancher, taut and angry, stepped in. He crossed to the center of the room, halted, hands on hips.

"Well—spit it out! What's your price?"

"For the letter?"

"Hell, yes—why else would I be here? You've got a price, I expect."

Shawn nodded.

"How much?"

"Not money," Starbuck said quietly. "All you've got to do is go to the sheriff, tell him the truth."

The rancher swore wildly. "I knew I was a damned fool —letting you in on it!"

"If you hadn't," Shawn said in a dry voice, "you wouldn't be the hero everybody's talking about."

Underwood stared, then shrugged and, moving to the bed, sat down. "Can't see why you're getting so hard-nosed about this. Means nothing to you. . . . I'm willing to pay for your help. Worth five hundred in gold—your help and that letter."

"Lot of money," Starbuck said. "But I'm not Rutter or the others."

The rancher groaned. "You've got a price—same as every man. This holier-than-thou act of yours isn't fooling

107

me. Let's cut it and get down to hard cases. Five hundred's not enough—all right—how much?"

"You heard the price."

Underwood rose from the bed in a sudden burst of rage. "Why, you saddletramp! You think you can blackmail me? I—I'll—"

"Expect I could," Shawn said calmly. "Be real easy to do—but I'm not figuring on it. All I want is for folks to know the truth about you. Afterwards, if they want to overlook it, forget all about what you've done, it'll be fine with me. I just think they've got a right to all the facts about the man who's wanting to be their governor."

"The facts! I'd be crazy to tell—"

"You don't know for sure how they'd take it. Could be they'd stand by you."

The rancher relaxed slightly. "You think they'd do that —stand by me?"

"Odds seem pretty fair to me. Far as I'm concerned they can go on thinking you're a hero—and I reckon you've done some good for the country."

Underwood was silent for a full minute. Finally he shook his head. "No, I just can't risk it. . . . Too much to lose."

"Heard you say that before," Shawn said, his voice hardening. "Back there in the bank when we went up against Rutter and his bunch. . . . You were to side me."

"I know, I know," Underwood murmured. "Couldn't seem to make myself do it—face those guns—"

"Takes guts to lie, too. You've got plenty of that kind."

The rancher lifted his hands, allowed them to fall. "Didn't actually plan it that way, Starbuck. You've got to believe that. Everybody just sort of latched onto the idea —me being there alone. Before I knew it the word was going around fast. . . . You know how things like that spread."

"Didn't hear you bothering to straighten anybody out on it. . . . Makes no difference. Killing a man—good or bad—is nothing to be proud of. One thing I'd like to know, however."

Underwood frowned, resumed his place on the bed. "What's that?"

"Rutter. . . . Did he try to run for it after I left, or did you shoot him down to keep him from talking? Way it's worked out, none of that bunch pulling that paymaster holdup is alive now but you."

"He was going to run for it—"

"With a bullet in his side and bleeding like a stuck hog —and you holding a gun on him?"

"He tried to get away," Underwood insisted dully. "It's the gospel truth."

Starbuck shifted his legs. "I'm hoping so. You're going to have hell living with the thought of it, if it wasn't."

"Not worried about that," the rancher said, regaining a grip on himself. "What about that letter? I've got to have it. Let's come to some kind of terms."

Shawn shrugged. "You've heard mine—and I won't track over them again. You take a walk with me to the sheriff's office—"

"Abrams isn't in town—"

"A deputy'll do. Moment you start talking, I'll hand you the letter and move on."

"I'd rather wait for Abrams—no use bringing the whole town in on it at first. Give me the letter now and you've got my word I'll wait for Abrams, tell him the whole story minute he shows up."

"Afraid that's not enough."

"My word's good to plenty of others!" Underwood exploded defensively. "You think you've got me by the short hair, don't you? Mister, you're wrong as hell! I've got a lot of friends around here—friends that owe me favors. If I want, all I need do is walk out into that street, tell a dozen men that you're setting up here trying to rawhide me into paying you off for something, and in less time than it takes to skin a snake, they'll have you swinging from a tree!"

"Maybe so," Shawn replied, "but during that time I'll get some talking done. And I'll manage to get that letter into somebody's hands who'll be curious enough or honest enough to see that it's delivered. Then what?"

"They'd give it to me first."

"Doubt that—it being addressed to the U.S. Marshal or the Sheriff."

The rancher was studying Starbuck narrowly. "You open it?"

"No. Leave that up to the law."

Sam Underwood came again to his feet, stretched forth his hand. "Mind if I take a look at it?"

"Not for you, either."

Anger again flamed in the rancher's eyes. "I can see there's no sense trying to reason with you. I'm willing to treat you right, but you won't listen. What do you aim to do next?"

"Only thing I can. If you won't go to the law, I'll take

109

the letter to the sheriff—or maybe on to the marshal in Santa Fe."

Underwood mopped at the sweat beading his forehead. "Supposing I raise the ante—say to a thousand. That's a hell of a lot of money."

"Won't argue that."

"A thousand would buy a man most anything he had a hankering for—could even get himself started in the cattle business."

"You're wasting your breath, Underwood. I'm not about to change my mind."

"Goddammit! What's the matter with you? This thing don't mean anything far as you're concerned. You don't even live in the Territory! What difference it make to you who or what—"

"Man can't turn his back on a wrong just because it's not in his own yard. Was taught that. . . . Expect you were, too."

"Ain't the point. . . . Way I see it, you're meddling in where you don't belong, mixing yourself up in business that sure ain't none of your business. . . . Fact is, nosing around like you are could get you killed."

Shawn stirred, smiled faintly. Now came the threats. Sam Underwood was trying everything in a desperate effort to get his hands on Guy Rutter's letter.

"You think I was bulling you about getting a dozen men to work you over on my say-so? Be no problem at all, and there'd be no questions asked by Sheriff Abrams —or anybody else. You're a stranger here. I'm not. This is my town, my Territory. What I'd tell them would—"

"You won't yell for help," Starbuck broke in wearily. "Too big a chance of that letter getting into the wrong hands—for you."

"Not that at all. Just don't want to cause you a lot of trouble."

"Trouble's yours, not mine."

The rancher swore angrily again. "You're a plain fool, Starbuck! Work with me and I'll make you a big man around here. A thousand dollars to start. Then when I'm governor, I'll put you in as chief of the mounted police. That's one of the promises I've made folks—that I'd organize a mounted police force, like the Texas Rangers. You'd make a good chief. . . . A thousand in gold on top of that. I'll put it in writing if you say so."

Shawn got to his feet slowly, almost lazily. "You're a hard man to convince, Underwood—and I'm tired of

110

wrangling. Nothing's changed. If you're not going along with my terms—get out."

The rancher stared. His face whitened and his lips worked convulsively as rage swept through him. "Nobody talks to me that way—"

"Could be they never had the chance, or maybe they had too big of an axe to grind. Happens you don't count with me one way or another. I'm looking for nothing— just want to see the right thing done."

"The hell! Who're you to say what's right and what's wrong?"

"Already asked myself that question. Man can only go by what he knows inside himself is right."

"According to what *he* thinks is right. . . . Could be you're wrong, Starbuck—dead wrong! Well, I'm promising you this: it's a hundred yards down the street from here to Abrams' office. You'll never get there alive."

"We'll see," Shawn said coolly. "So long, Mr. Underwood."

The rancher's eyes flared, and then wheeling stiffly, he crossed the room, yanked open the door, and disappeared into the dark hallway.

◎ 20 ◎

Starbuck gazed at the opening through which the rancher had vanished. Moving forward, he pushed the panel closed and stood for a time with his eyes on the knob.

As far as the sheriff was concerned, there was nothing he could do until morning, and possibly not even then if Abrams had not returned to the settlement. And he would not risk taking the matter to the deputy—Harvey, or whatever his name was. He appeared to be one who would succumb quickly to Sam Underwood's blandishments and persuasion.

But there was no ignoring the rancher's final threat. The man, a deceptively ruthless one, pushed to the extreme by the possibility of seeing his political ambitions collapse in personal disaster, would doubtless act quickly; and with the influence he was in a position to wield, he'd find many men to do his bidding regardless of its nature.

Thus it would be foolhardy to take Underwood's promise lightly. Brazen as it might seem, the chances were that hidden marksmen would keep him from ever reaching Sheriff Abrams' office; moreover, now that he gave it thought, the likelihood of his even getting out of the hotel was probably growing slimmer with each passing moment.

Starbuck swore impatiently. All he wanted was to find Ben; instead he'd gotten sidetracked, and the whole purpose of his being in the Territory was lost in the shuffle. Best thing he could do was climb out of the jam he was in fast, get back to his original purpose.

Take first things first. It was dangerous to hang around Las Vegas any longer; the letter was addressed primarily to the U.S. Marshal who maintained an office in Santa Fe. The solution, therefore, was to slip out of town immediately without the rancher being aware of it, swing by the ranch in the hope that Henry Smith had returned, talk with him, and then, regardless of the outcome, ride on to Santa Fe and deliver Rutter's letter. . . .

It was the only sensible way to handle the situation. Leaning down, he drew aside the curtains, looked out into the street. There were still a few persons abroad and a guard had been positioned in front of the shattered window of the bank. Business in the saloons had not slackened.

Shawn's glance paused on three men standing in a close group a short distance beyond the Gold Dollar. One of them was Underwood. He grinned tightly. The rancher was doing as expected; he was already busy recruiting those dozen men he had mentioned. . . . He was being blackmailed, he'd tell them; there was a personal letter involved, one that belonged to him despite what it said on its face. Sam Underwood, hero, would be able to convince them of anything.

Reaching up, Shawn drew the sun-stiffened shade and turned to the bed. Pulling back the patch quilt, and using one of the two pillows, he shaped the bed clothing into the semblance of a sleeping person. That done, he took up his saddlebags, pulled on his hat, and moving to the door, opened it cautiously.

There was no one in the hall. Although acting swiftly, Underwood had not yet had time to station a sentry in the hotel. Stepping out, he closed the panel silently, locked it and thrust the key into his pocket.

Making his way down the corridor, he came to a second hall crossing at right angles. He turned left into it, followed along its narrow channel to the rear of the building. A door faced him at its end, and again cautious, he cracked it slightly. A low sigh passed his lips when he saw that it led into the yard that separated the hotel from the stable.

It was what he looked for. Stepping out onto the landing, he threw his glance to all directions, saw no one. Considerable noise was coming from the street, now on the opposite side of the structure, but he felt he had nothing to worry about from that point; it was unlikely anyone could see the yard.

Holding his saddlebags, he crossed the weed-littered hard pack to the barn, slipped inside. The hostler's quarters lay to his left. Shawn eased up to the door and peered inside. The room was empty. The hostler likely was out in the street savoring the excitement.

113

Hurrying on down the runway he located the chestnut. His gear had been slung across a nearby rack, and grabbing up the blanket, he saddled and bridled the gelding in quick, efficient moves.

That finished, he backed the horse into the clear, again stopped at the hostler's quarters. Stepping inside, he laid a silver dollar and the key to his room on the dust-covered table and withdrew. . . . He was square now with the Exchange Hotel and the stablekeeper.

A few moments later he was astride the chestnut and making his way through the deep shadows along the edge of the yard, toward the street. The road east lay at the opposite end of town, and he would be forced to cross over. He'd do that well down, beyond the view of anyone standing near the hotel or the saloons.

He pulled up, leaned forward, searching the night-shrouded shrubbery for any indication of an alley or similar passageway that would permit him to reach that point without going all the way to the street. There seemed to be none; a rail fence ran the full depth of the adjacent property.

He started to come about, have a look at the land behind the stable, thinking perhaps to find an open field. He pulled up short as the sounds of someone approaching caught his attention, sent a warning racing through him.

"On the front, Sam said. . . ."

In the broad shadow cast by an aged cottonwood, Starbuck hung motionless and prayed the gelding also would make no move.

Two figures came from the front of the hotel. They walked with care but the gravel crunched solidly beneath their tread. Reaching the end of the walk they turned, headed for the rear entrance to the hostelry.

"We could've gone through the lobby," the smaller of the pair said in a grumbling tone. "Old Pankey'd be asleep this time of night. Always is."

"Somebody else might've seen us—and Sam said we was to be quiet, do it without no fuss."

The chestnut shifted, stamped a hoof. Instantly the men halted, wheeled.

"Who's that?" the taller one called.

Both pulled away from the wall of the building, edged deeper into the yard. Weak moonlight glinted feebly on the pistols they had drawn.

"Nobody special," Shawn replied, his hand sliding down to where it rested on the butt of his own weapon. "No need for that hardware. . . . One of you the hostler?"

"Hell, no," the tall man said in disgust. "You coming or going?"

"Little of both, depending on how you look at it. Know where the hostler'll be?"

"Probably down at Kaseman's saloon. Where he is most of the time. You're a-wanting to stable your horse, best thing you can do is see to it yourself. He ain't apt to show up till every saloon in town's closed."

"Obliged," Starbuck said, and nudging the gelding gently, doubled back over his tracks toward the wide doors of the stable.

Entering, he halted in the odorous blackness, looked over his shoulder. The men were just going into the hotel through the same door he had used earlier. He waited out a long two minutes, assuring himself the pair would not reappear, and then cut back through the stable's entrance into the yard.

He'd best waste no more time scouting for a back way out of town—there was none left, not with Underwood's friends already moving in on him. Likely there were others in the front watching the window and the lobby door. The rancher evidently had decided not to wait until morning to act; his own hunch to pull out had been a good one.

Holding the chestnut to a walk, and again in the deep shadows, he made his way to the street. Turning sharply right, he rode along the shoulder, deserted in this fringe area, until he came to the last building. Then, touching the big horse with spurs, he crossed and swung onto the road that led to Underwood's ranch.

"Gone!"

The word ripped from Sam Underwood's lips with all the suddenness of a pistol shot.

Standing in the darkness behind the bank, the tall puncher nodded his head vigorously.

"Yessir, gone. When we got inside his room all we found was the bed fixed up so's it looked like somebody was sleeping in it. . . . Only it wasn't nobody."

The rancher swore harshly. "Now, when in the hell could he have got out? Wasn't no more'n thirty minutes after I left him that I sent you two over there."

"Must've done it right after you left," the short rider said.

"You sure he ain't in one of the other rooms? Could've played it smart—changed."

"We got Pankey on his feet, asked him that. Said no.

Far as he knew that Starbuck fellow was in the room he'd rented—Number Four."

"You look in the others?"

"Sure did—them that wasn't rented, which most of them ain't. Never found nobody."

"Then he's here in town somewhere, hiding," Sam Underwood said with conviction. "Got to root him out."

"We checked all the saloons. Couldn't spot him. And I ain't about to go opening them doors on the second floor of the Gold Dollar. Man could get his head blowed off doing that."

Again the rancher swore, deeply, fiercely. He hadn't expected Starbuck to run for cover, had figured he'd wait in the hotel until morning to see Abrams. Starbuck was no fool. He'd underestimated him—had all along, he guessed.

"What you want us to do now, Sam?"

The rancher shook his head, walked slowly for the street. "Got to do some thinking. Wherever he's holed up, the place he'll be trying to get to in the morning is the sheriff's office. Got to keep him from doing that."

"Now, how you—"

"Charley, I want you to take your rifle and get up on the roof of Hayden's Feed Store. Keep hid so's nobody'll see you. . . . Tuck, you plant yourself in that empty store building down the street from Hayden's."

The tall man drew a loud breath. "You mean you're wanting us to shoot him right out there in broad daylight?"

"What an outlaw like him deserves," Underwood said. "Anyway, won't anybody see you if you're careful. He'll line out for Abrams early. Street'll probably be empty, and I'll be standing on the porch of the Exchange—"

"Why don't you just go ahead yourself, Sam, do the shooting?"

"Be better if I don't, after all that killing I did this evening. Can't have folks thinking I'm gun crazy. Like I said —I'll be on the porch of the hotel. When I see him drop, I'll run to him, get them papers he stole from me. You two can sort of fade off, come into the street farther down —like you'd just heard the shots, was wondering what they was all about—"

"I'd as soon as folks knowed it was me that done it— shooting an outlaw like him," Tuck said. "Might make some around here show me a little respect instead of laughing at me and looking down on me the way they do."

"However you want it," Underwood said impatiently. "If you don't want folks knowing, I can say I saw a rider

116

leaving town hell for leather, that I think he was the one who did it."

Charley scuffed at the dirt with the toe of his boot. "I ain't sure, Sam," he mumbled hesitantly. "Comes to shooting a man—bushwhacking him—wish we'd find him tonight so's—"

"Wish't we could've found that jasper we bumped into there at the stable," Tuck said. "I'll bet he seen that Starbuck fellow, and could've told us where he went."

Sam Underwood had come to stiff attention. "What jasper?"

"Some bird we seen back of the hotel when we first got there. Was looking for Smitty, that old soak that runs the stable. Said he—"

"You get a good look at him?"

"Hardly none. Was setting his horse under that big cottonwood."

"What about the horse—you see it?"

"Some. . . . Was big, know that. Think maybe it was a bay."

"Chestnut. Fourteen, fifteen hands high. Had white stockings and a blazed face?"

"Reckon that was the one. Where'd you see—"

"You damned fools!" Underwood snapped in disgust. "That was the man you were looking for."

Charley straightened up in surprise. Tuck pulled off his hat, scratched at his head. "It was? Well, we wasn't looking for no horse."

"Reckon it could've been at that," Charley said thoughtfully. "If I'd a guessed, I'd have taken a closer look at him. . . . Did go back to the stable later. Thought maybe he'd still be there. Aimed to ask him if he'd seen somebody—"

"And him and the horse were both gone," the rancher finished.

"Sure was. Couldn't find hide or hair of them."

"How long ago was this?"

"Hour, maybe. No more'n that."

Underwood stirred wearily. He should have known better than to line up a couple of bronc stompers like Charley and Tuck to do the job for him, but then it was a touchy situation and he didn't have much choice. They were stupid enough to do what he told them, and not smart enough to ask any questions.

Maybe it didn't matter. Maybe it was better this way. Starbuck was clever—he figured a move would be made to take Rutter's letter from him, so he ducked out, planning

117

to lay low until his chances improved. Safest bet would be for him to get out of town. . . . He might even head for Santa Fe and the U.S. Marshal—and then get clear out of the country.

Of course—that's just what he'd done. He was on his horse, all mounted and ready to ride when Charley and Tuck ran into him. He wouldn't have saddled up and all if what he had in mind was to just change places in town.

But he wouldn't go straight to Santa Fe. He had some kind of an idea that Henry Smith was the long-lost brother he'd been hunting for. . . . Seemed mighty important that he find him. He wouldn't head for Santa Fe until he had first stopped by the ranch, had a talk with Henry. . . . That was it. That's what he was doing.

"Get your horses," Underwood said in a sudden, harsh way. "Meet me at the south end of town in thirty minutes. . . . Charley, you stop by Abrams, get yourself a deputy's badge out of his desk drawer—I'll explain to the sheriff later."

"Yessir, Sam. . . . Where we going?"

"My place," the rancher replied. "That's where we'll find Starbuck."

◎ 21 ◎

Starbuck rode into the ranch shortly after sunrise. Leaving the chestnut at one of the hitchracks, he went immediately to Tom Gage's cabin. He was under no illusion about Sam Underwood; it wouldn't take the rancher long to discover he was not in Las Vegas, and probably even less time to figure he'd head for the ranch to see Henry Smith before riding on to Santa Fe.

Thus the minutes were at a premium unless he wished to wait and have a showdown. He would as soon avoid such. He had no personal quarrel with the man—at least one serious enough to warrant bloodshed, and, too, he was thinking of Holly. Bleak moments were ahead for her when she learned the man she idolized was not all she thought, and he had no desire to add further to her heartbreak.

Smith should have returned, he thought as he pushed open the door of Gage's quarters; he'd see him, have a talk, and then if it was the usual false lead he'd come to accept as almost inevitable, he'd line out for Santa Fe. But if Smith did prove to be Ben—well, he'd decide then what to do.

The old foreman was sitting on the edge of the bed rubbing at his whiskered face as Shawn came in. He glanced up, grinned.

"Back, eh? Good to see you."

Starbuck nodded. "Smith come in?"

"Sure did. Yesterday—late. . . . Hear Sam had hisself quite a whingding in Vegas. Them stinking sidewinders. Knowed they was no good the day I first laid eyes on them."

Shawn, about to return to the yard, make his way to the bunkhouse, paused in surprise. "How'd you know about it?"

Gage began to pull on his clothing. "The little gal— Holly. Got in early—her and Ira Cameron's womenfolk. Was so worked up and near busting her buttons about what her pa'd done, she couldn't wait to tell her ma and us all about it. Cameron had one of his hands drive them in his surrey. . . . Sam come in, too?"

"No," Starbuck said. "Be here soon, I expect."

Gage stood up, stamped his feet into his boots, began to close his shirt. "That gal is sure proud of Sam. He really do all she says—shoot it out with them jaspers and such?"

Shawn was silent for a long minute. Finally, "Expect she's telling it the way her pa told it to her."

The old foreman paused, studied Starbuck with his shrewd eyes. After a bit he resumed dressing. "Never figured Sam had that kind of spunk in him. . . . How'd it happen you wasn't in on it?"

"What did Holly say about me?"

"That you'd gone over to the saloon for a drink, left Sam by hisself."

The corners of Shawn's mouth pulled down into a wry smile, and then he shrugged. . . . Let it pass. It didn't really matter.

"Like to see Smith soon as I can," he said, getting off the subject.

"Help yourself. He'll be in the bunkhouse with the rest of the boys. Whole bunch'll be going in for chow in a minute. You could see him, do your eating at the same time." Once more Gage hesitated, considered Starbuck thoughtfully. "Something bothering you, son? You're acting plenty spooked."

"Hard ride. Expect I'm a bit on the wore-out side. Just want to see Henry Smith, move on if it turns out he's not my brother."

"Just like that, eh? Was figuring you to hang around for a spell. Didn't you sign on with Sam—that there special job—"

"Quit last night," Starbuck said, moving to the window. Several of the punchers were in the yard, standing around sleepily, yawning, stretching, having a first smoke.

"Any of those men Henry?" he asked.

Gage crowded up to his side, scanned the hard pack. "Nope, ain't one of them. . . . There—that's Henry coming out the bunkhouse now. One wearing a red-checkered shirt."

Starbuck pivoted swiftly to the door of the cabin, stepped out into the yard, quick, hard tension building within him. Henry Smith was dark and a stubble that covered his cheeks and chin looked blue.

Shawn's hopes rose. He could be Ben. . . . Built a lot like Hiram Starbuck—actually looked something like him. . . . Those big hands, that square-cut face. . . . Starbuck's pulses quickened, began to hammer as he strode toward the man. . . . Maybe he'd finally come to the end of his quest; perhaps this was the finish—here in the yard of a ranch where trouble was racing to overtake him.

He reached the front of the bunkhouse. Smith had stepped to the edge of the landing, was gazing at the hills to the east.

"Henry Smith?" Shawn said hesitantly as he pulled up a pace or two away.

The trail boss turned lazily. "That's me, I reckon."

Dark eyes—not blue. . . . But maybe the color had changed through the years.

"You want me for something?"

Shawn caught himself, said, "Yes. . . . My name's Starbuck."

Smith waited, his face quizzical. "So?"

"That name mean anything to you?"

"Nope, can't say as it does. It supposed to?"

A ponderous, weighty disappointment settled over Shawn. "Was hoping it would. I'm looking for my brother. Name's Ben. Was hoping you might be him."

"Ain't got no kin," Smith said. "I'm purely a orphan." He half smiled, looked closer at Starbuck, a suspicious glint in his eyes. "You funning me?"

"No. . . . Man up in Kansas said you sort of fit the description I gave of Ben—what I have, anyway. Rode down here to see you, thinking maybe—"

"Well, I'm real sorry you had yourself a long ride for nothing. I sure ain't your brother. I ain't nobody's brother. Like I said, I'm a orphan."

Shawn, clinging to one final strand of hope, stepped up onto the landing. Bitter as Ben had been when he ran off, it was possible he still entertained the same feelings about the family name and would refuse to admit any relationship. . . . There was that one proof he could neither hide nor deny.

"You looking for something special?" Smith asked mildly.

Shawn's eyes were on the rider's face, searching for that telltale scar over the left brow. . . . There were

121

lines, cut there by endless days in the sun and wind, but no memento of that day in the rocks now so many years in the past.

Shoulders going down, Starbuck fell back. "No, I guess you're not him. Maybe you don't even look like him, I don't know for sure."

"Well, he's a right lucky soul," Smith drawled, "not taking after a ugly critter like me. Ain't you got no idea a'tall where you can find him?"

"None," Shawn answered, staring off across the hard pack. "Don't even know what name he goes by. Doesn't call himself Ben Starbuck—sure of that."

Henry Smith whistled softly. "Mister, you've picked yourself one hell of a smoke trail to be riding! Why, a man could follow it till Kingdom Come and not find what he's looking for."

"I'll find him," Shawn said wearily. "Got to."

"If you're lucky—and he ain't dead," the rider said. "Well, I'm hoping you do. He all the kin you got?"

Starbuck nodded. "Trailing herds, you run into a lot of people. You ever remember seeing a man that might've been him? He'd probably look a lot like you—build and such. Eyes more'n likely are blue. . . . Main thing, he's got a scar over the left one."

"So that's what you was doing—looking for a scar!" the trail boss said with a wide grin. "Figured there for a bit I maybe had lice or something." He sobered, scrubbed the stubble on his chin, his glance on the rest of the crew now drifting toward the kitchen for the morning meal.

"When you first mentioned what you was after, I did recollect a fellow, but I ain't one to send no man out on a snipe hunt."

"Only way I'll ever find Ben is to ride down every prospect I hear about. Been doing it for quite a spell. Another failure won't matter—and this time it just might be him. . . . Who is this man and where'd you see him?"

"Name of Jim Ivory. Punches cows for the Box C outfit, down Arizona way—the Mogollon country. Fellow once said we looked enough alike to be twins."

Revived hope stirred within Shawn. "How long ago was this?"

"Couple, three years I reckon since I seen Jim. Reckon he's still there if he ain't gone and got hisself killed in a poker game. A plain dang fool when it come to cards. Carries a deck right in his pocket. Every time he sets down, out comes them cards. If he can't talk some of the boys into playing with him, why, he just plays by hisself."

"Box C," Starbuck murmured. "The Mogollon country. Was through there about a year ago—on my way to Tucson. Didn't stop. Remember there was a town by the name of Lynchburg."

"Your rememberer's good. Box C's about twenty miles west. Big spread. You won't have no trouble finding it."

The cook began to hammer on his iron bar, summoning the stragglers. Smith yawned, grinned, said, "Reckon he means us. I ain't even got around to washing the night off my face, but I ain't minding it if nobody else does. . . . Come on, Starbuck, we'd best be getting there."

"Go ahead," Shawn said, extending his hand to the rider. "Appreciate what you told me about this Jim Ivory, and sorry if I bothered you some."

"No bother—only wish't I did belong to somebody. Ain't you eating with us?"

"Not this morning," Shawn replied. The last thing he wanted was to sit down at Sam Underwood's table, eat his food. "So long. . . ."

"Adios," Henry Smith said, stepping off the landing and heading for the kitchen. "Luck."

Shawn turned, moved toward the chestnut waiting patiently at the hitchrack. *Tot up one more failure,* he thought, but the slash of disappointment was not so deep as once it was; too many other promising leads had ended this way.

He glanced over to Gage's cabin. He would have liked to see the old foreman before he rode on, to express his thanks, but he'd be with the crew now, having his breakfast. Just as well he wasn't handy. Tom's eyes had told him he wasn't swallowing the story Holly Underwood brought back from Las Vegas—not entirely, anyway. He'd ask questions, sharp and probing—and Shawn knew he couldn't lie to the old man.

And Holly. . . . He didn't want to see her again, either. Her estimation of him after what her father had told her would be at its lowest point. He regretted leaving her with that belief, but that was the way it had to be. Someday she'd know the truth and perhaps think better of him. At the present, however, he doubted if she would even speak to him, much less tell him farewell and wish him luck.

He reached the chestnut, jerked the reins loose, prepared to swing up. He froze as his eyes reached to the corner of the bunkhouse beyond the gelding.

Underwood, on a borrowed horse, flanked by two men —one of whom wore a deputy sheriff's star—was coming around the end of the building and entering the yard.

◎ 22 ◎

Momentarily startled, the rancher pulled up short, the horses of the men with him shouldering against his own at the sudden stop. Shawn recognized the pair; they were the two he'd encountered back at the Exchange Hotel. Pivoting fast, he drew his pistol, stepped in behind the chestnut so that his back was to the corral fence.

Underwood, recovered, wagged his head. "Put it away, Starbuck. You're on my land now."

Shawn cast a fleeting glance to the yard behind him. Everyone was inside the house at breakfast. Resting his arms on the gelding's saddle, holding the gun steady on the three men, he said, "Makes no difference to me."

"Should. You'll never leave here alive unless I say the word. . . . Now, all you have to do is drop that letter on the ground—then you can mount up, ride out."

"Letter stays with me. Taking it to the marshal in Santa Fe."

"Like hell you are!" Underwood shouted suddenly. "I sing out—my whole crew'll be crawling over you. Give it up. You ain't got a chance."

"Long as my first bullet's aimed at your heart, I have."

Over in the direction of the main house a door slammed. Holly's voice cried, "Papa—you're here!"

Starbuck remained rigid, not daring to turn and look around. He could hear the girl running. The door slapped again, this time with less abandon. Mrs. Underwood, probably. . . . Coming to welcome the hero.

Abruptly Holly was moving by him, her steps slowing as an expression of bewilderment crossed her face. She halted just beyond Shawn, stared first at her father, then at Starbuck, back to Underwood once more.

"What—what's the matter?"

"Just a little trouble between me and Starbuck, honey,"

124

the rancher replied. "You and your mother best get back in the house. Take the Camerons with you."

The girl whirled to Shawn, eyes blazing. "What's the meaning of this? How dare you point that gun at my father—right here in his own yard!"

Starbuck's face was wooden. "Ask him. Maybe he'll tell you why."

"Tell me what?"

Shawn shrugged. The girl looked to her father. "What is it? This over what happened in Vegas?"

"Part of it," Underwood said. "Go on—do what I tell you, Holly. No place for you here."

"I won't!" the girl cried stubbornly. "Not until he puts that gun away and I know what this is about. . . . Was he in with those other outlaws—the ones you had to shoot?"

"In a way—"

"I thought so!" Holly said triumphantly, moving toward Shawn. "My father had to shoot them, stop them from robbing his bank—and you're here to get even. That's it, isn't it?"

Starbuck's eyes never strayed from Underwood. "That what you want her to believe—a lie?"

The rancher, slumped on his saddle, merely stared. The two men beside him remained silent, watchful. Some of the assurance had faded from Holly's manner, however. She studied her father, a frown pulling at her brow.

"I don't understand. . . . What does he mean? What lie? You said he wasn't there, that he'd gone to the saloon for a—" Abruptly she whirled to Starbuck. "Wasn't that the truth? Didn't you go to the saloon?"

Shawn nodded.

"Then it happened just like Papa told me, didn't it?"

Starbuck remained quiet. There was movement back and around him now, hushed, careful. The crew, attracted by the sound of voices, had come out, were circling, boxing him in.

"Well, didn't it?" Holly demanded.

"You'll have to ask your pa," Starbuck said wearily.

"I'm asking you!"

"And you'll get no answer."

Holly smiled, bobbed her head in satisfaction. "Just as I thought. You're after vengeance. I knew my father wouldn't lie."

"Mr. Underwood," a voice cut in from the far left side of the yard, "I got him covered from here. Akins' drawing a bead on him from the feed shed. What you want us to do?"

A hard grin parted the rancher's lips. "Don't let him move. . . . I say the word—shoot."

"You're a dead man if you do," Shawn warned softly. "I don't want gunplay, but it'll come if you force my hand. Best you call them off."

Underwood considered Starbuck's set features for a long minute while the tense hush in the yard deepened. He shook his head. "Hold off, boys. Jump him and he's liable to do something crazy—and there's womenfolk around." The rancher shifted heavily on the saddle and glared at Shawn. "What's it to be? We just going to stand here all day?"

"Maybe was we to find out what this is all about we could straighten things up," Tom Gage's voice broke in from somewhere behind Starbuck.

A trickle of relief began to run through Shawn. Gage was one man in the yard he felt he could trust. Sam Underwood shifted again.

"Keep out of it, Tom."

"No, reckon not. We got a standoff here that'll probably end up with somebody dead," the old foreman said, moving up until he was directly opposite Shawn. "Sure don't want that. . . . Now, since ain't either one of you willing to talk, maybe somebody else is. How about you, Charley? Say—is that there a deputy star you're wearing? Didn't know Abrams was that hard up for help."

Charley displayed a self-conscious grin. "Aw, I ain't no real deputy, Tom. Mr. Underwood told me to get this here badge—"

"Shut up, you damned fool!" the rancher snapped.

Gage considered Sam Underwood narrowly. "Keep talking, Charley."

"About what? I don't know nothing much," the rider said. "He hired Tuck and me to sneak into that there fellow's room at the hotel. Was supposed to get a envelope with some papers in it. Something he was blackmailing Mr. Underwood with. . . . Fellow got away before we could grab the papers, so we followed him here."

The foreman shifted his attention to Shawn. "You got some papers, like Charley says?"

"Got a letter. No blackmail on my part. It was written by Rutter. He meant for it to be turned over to the U.S. Marshal if he got killed."

"And you're aiming to deliver it but Sam's against your doing it—that what this is all about?"

Starbuck said, "Covers it. Matter for the law."

Gage glanced to the rancher. "Sam, you going to say anything?"

"He was wanting us to shoot the big jasper," Tuck volunteered. "Said we wasn't to let him take that there letter he's carrying to the sheriff. Just had to have it."

A faint gasp came from Holly. She turned, started walking toward her mother. The foreman frowned. "What's that letter all about, Sam?"

Underwood's features were set, grim. His eyes hardened and filled suddenly with a wild, desperate light as he looked around the yard.

"The hell with all of you!" he shouted and drew his pistol fast. He fired point-blank at Starbuck and in the same instant jammed spurs into the horse sending the animal plunging straight at Shawn.

Starbuck leaped away and fired his weapon as the rancher got off a second shot. Underwood's first bullet was wide but the second ripped through the sleeve of Shawn's brush jacket, thudded into a corral pole behind him. Starbuck crouched, prepared to fire again. There was no need. The rancher was sagging forward on his saddle, one hand clutching his shoulder. Back near the house Holly was screaming and men were closing in from all sides.

"Everybody just hold up a minute now!"

Tom Gage's words sounded above the confusion. The thudding of boots died. Shawn relaxed gently. The foreman stepped forward, grasped the reins of Underwood's nervous horse.

"Couple of you men—help Sam down. . . . He ain't hurt bad." Gage swung about to face Starbuck, extended his hand. "I'll be taking that letter—see if it's worth all this ruckus. It is, I'll see the marshal gets—"

"No!" Underwood groaned, his head coming up with a jerk. His eyes came to a level, saw Holly and his wife running toward him, met also the wondering glances of the crew. Abruptly his head lowered again.

"Let him see it," he muttered in absolute defeat. "Let them all see it. Tell them everything—the whole damned mess. . . ."

Starbuck holstered his gun. "Nobody sees it," he said quietly. "Nobody but the U.S. Marshal. If he wants to do anything about it, it's up to him."

Holly and her mother rushed by. Together they pushed away the two punchers supporting Underwood, assumed the task themselves. The rancher, a puzzled look on his face, stared at Shawn, and then once more he dropped his eyes.

"Don't matter. . . . I'm done with thinking and worrying and sweating over things. . . . Going to the marshal myself, put it all in his hands. . . . Won't have it setting on my mind then."

"Best thing you can do—" Starbuck began.

"You get out of here!" Holly screamed at him, whirling. "You've shot him—hurt him—isn't that enough?"

Shawn lowered his head. "I'm sorry. I—"

"Sorry! What good's that? You might have killed him! If you don't leave right now, I'll get a gun myself and—"

"I'm going," Starbuck said quietly and stepped back to the chestnut.

Swinging onto the saddle, he wheeled about, rode slowly from the yard, not allowing his glance to touch any of those in the yard. There was no point in making any gesture of farewell—he knew he would get none in return.

Gaining the land swell to the south of the ranch, he paused, looked back. Sam Underwood, with his women assisting, was just entering the house. Gage and the punchers were moving off, preparing to take up the day's work. Two riders were turning into the trees west of the buildings. . . . Tuck and Charley returning to Las Vegas.

Shawn heaved a long sigh, reached into his shirt and procured Guy Rutter's letter. He read again the writing on its crumpled surface: *U.S. Marshal or Sheriff*. . . . He'd been both judge and jury where Sam Underwood was concerned, and it had been an uncomfortable and far from pleasant experience. But it was finished. The rancher had finally faced up to himself—and would now have to meet his obligations to others.

Taking the letter between his fingers, he began to tear it into small bits, allowing the light, pinon-scented breeze to scatter the scraps across the slope. Underwood had made peace with himself, would now with the law—there was no need for Rutter's denunciation.

Nor was there any necessity for him to think any more about it, or the friends he'd made and lost and would again someday, perhaps, regain when the truth was out. He needed now to put his mind on the ride ahead—a ride that would take him into the Mogollon country of Arizona where he would look up a man called Jim Ivory. . . . He just might be Ben. . . .